T0146613

THE
IMPOSSIBLE
EARTH

THE
IMPOSSIBLE
EARTH

*What If Tomorrow's Yesterday
Wasn't Today?*

JOHN KNIGHT

THE IMPOSSIBLE EARTH
WHAT IF TOMORROW'S YESTERDAY WASN'T TODAY?

iUniverse books may be ordered through booksellers or by contacting:

iUniverse
1663 Liberty Drive
Bloomington, IN 47403
www.iuniverse.com
1-800-Authors (1-800-288-4677)

ISBN: 978-1-5320-3749-8 (sc)
ISBN: 978-1-5320-3750-4 (hc)
ISBN: 978-1-5320-3751-1 (e)

Library of Congress Control Number: 2017917871

Print information available on the last page.

iUniverse rev. date: 01/29/2018

ACKNOWLEDGEMENTS

The contents of this book
Could not have made it this far
Without the aid, creative inspiration,
And consistent support of
Kitten & Daggs!

Daggs, you have continued to believe in me,
Even when things seemed hopeless.

Kitten, my love, my fiancee
You never ceased to have unyielding faith in me
And, were it not for your initial interest,
And willingness to look at my work in progress,
There may not have even BEEN a book now.

My eternal thanks to you both!

Special thanks to Ashley Levine and Krystal Knight for allowing their ring personas (AshleyConda & Goddess Faith respectively) to be used/referenced during this story

DEDICATION

The inspired composition of this work
will forever be impacted by the tragic
loss of my dear friend Tali,
who died in hospital after suffering from a series of ailments,
finishing with a particularly aggressive form of cancer.

Tali suffered from Fanconi Anemia.
Subsequently, a portion of the proceeds
from the sale of this book
will be donated towards research to find a cure for this disease.

I am proud to do my part to honour the memory of
a very compassionate and powerful soul.

Forever in My Heart and Mind
May You Have Finally Found
Peace and Tranquility

Tali Rom
September 9, 1986 – April 6, 2015

CONTENTS

PROLOGUE

HOPE AND DESPAIR

New Email Received!

Date: Monday, October 20, 2014 17:21 (EST)
From: Miles Militis (friendly2afault@curiosity.com)
Subject: Re: Weekend Plans & Random Thoughts

Hey Angelique,

I got your latest e-mail. I'm sorry it has taken me so long to get back to you. It was quite a busy weekend, but I'm confident that Amber and I are on the verge of taking our relationship to the next level. She loves watching me work with my hands, so the renovation work at your place next weekend will really help me earn some brownie points!

It's a shame that Jack won't be able to be there with us; but I think it's very neat that he has the opportunity to work on a film about the history of things and Greek philosophers! You know me; I have been inspired to learn more about how things came to be, and why.

I have mixed feelings about how my day went today. On the one hand, I have a feeling that all of my hard work and willingness to take on overflow from other employees at the office is finally going to pay off. They are restructuring, and some jobs are opening up as a result. On the other hand…ugh…it is really not getting any better out there; not on the streets, not in the news, not on the transit system. There are just too many people riding transit and not enough vehicles to accommodate the load. Gas prices are insane, so driving isn't an appealing alternative either.

And then there are the news stories from around the world, and it just makes one wish they could remain ignorant of it. Unfortunately, I know better than to think that not knowing about something will impact its effect upon me and my life.

I'm sorry, my dearest and oldest friend, I am rambling now. I'm just tired, stressed, frustrated, and a bit disappointed at what this world has ended up becoming.

I will talk to you soon, if not by e-mail, then maybe by text. I think my data is running low for the month. However, use whatever format you prefer.

Sincerely,
Miles Militis

☺☺☺

YOU HAVE (1) NEW E-MAIL!

DATE: Tuesday, October 21, 2014 1:04pm (EST)
FROM: Angelique Lambros-Erebus (new.beginnings@
           visionary.com)
SUBJECT: RE: Weekend Plans & Random Thoughts (5)

Hello Miles,

I am fully aware of how busy things are for you right now, and could not be happier for you. You've got a steady job, and a girlfriend who clearly loves you; I've never seen you so happy, and I've known you for over 20 years now!

I *was* going to send a text instead, as you had recommended, but I felt I had more to say than a text message would hold, without becoming a multimedia message instead.

Yes, I think Jack would've really wanted to be there with us this weekend, but I'm so proud of him for pursuing his career, and going to such lengths to do so.

I know you are unhappy with your commute to and from work, and the news stories that you read about along the way. But the world isn't really that bad; I mean, it could be a lot worse. Mind you, I'm one to talk, aren't I? I'm always thinking of ways that the world could be better, if people just put their minds to it, and if they really dedicated themselves towards a common goal.

3

What if we could clean the air and be able to drink the water that we wade, swim, and sail upon? What if gas prices were fair and based on supply & demand? What if we could just...

Sorry Miles, I have to cut this e-mail short, I see the delivery van pulling into the driveway, which means that we should have all of the materials that we need for our reno work on the weekend. Then we just need to pick up a few things on the weekend that aren't available for delivery.

I really hope the rest of this week goes well for you, and look forward to hearing all about it over dinner on Friday evening.

From your supportive bestie!

Angelique

CHAPTER 1

THAT SPECIAL FEELING...

KALOS TROFI CAFE
1:26pm, Tuesday October 21ˢᵗ, 2014

"Angie, I just got a chance to read yer e-mail, by using the café's Wi-Fi; my data was lower than I realized, so had to wait until I could find other means to access your message. My first reaction to your...rather lofty viewpoints was less than positive. So I will sum up with: LOL! Yer dreaming, U R!" Miles texted to his friend during his lunch break. *"Perhaps that was not the most mature response"* he told himself. The week had gotten off to a bit of a rough start, and he was in the middle of a very busy day. *"But is that any excuse to respond so flippantly to a dear friend expressing herself openly?"* he wondered. Looking at his watch, he realized that he perhaps had taken too long to think about it, and was nearing the end of his lunch break. It wasn't a long journey back to the office, but he never liked to be late for anything, particularly work.

Miles Militis was a hard-working Caucasian male in his mid-thirties who worked very diligently at his job, and at keeping the work that he did interesting in order to maintain a high level of productivity and efficiency. However, he had a reputation for always finding time to be there for his friends, particularly ones that he'd known for as long as he had known Angelique.

Angelique Lambros-Erebus, wife of famous actor/writer/ philosopher Jack Erebus, has been friends with Miles for over 25 years. Her exposure to her husband's philosophical teachings and practices had helped broaden the scope of her own life and goals. This helped her to also better understand Miles' keen interest in learning about the history of things, why things are as they are, and how they came to be introduced to the world to begin with.

Unfortunately, she'd opted to open up to her best friend about her thoughts and viewpoints which would naturally lead in a different direction, regarding scientific philosophy, future technology, etc., at an inopportune time. She knew that this was a big week for him, but part of her was still saddened by the crass and cold response he had given to her e-mail. Another part of her realized that she'd clearly chosen the wrong time to express her thoughts and ideas on the subject. "He *told me that he was having a rough week, why did I think he'd have the time or patience to discuss such things? Why didn't I wait until he came over on the weekend?*" she asked herself.

"The weekend..." she repeated the thought softly to herself, then she remembered that she'd have to re-confirm that he was still available and willing to come over. "Are you still coming over on Saturday to help with renovations and such?" she texted.

It had started out as a cool, crisp morning, but had become relatively mild for downtown Toronto in late October. Miles felt comfortable enough to go out for lunch, without bringing a jacket. A part of him could have cared less about the temperature. He felt the breeze blowing between the skyscrapers that lined the street, and he found it rather invigorating as he headed back towards the office.

Miles was having a particularly good month, both in and out of work. He didn't fully grasp the whole modern science and experimental philosophy thing. A part of him didn't want to. He wasn't often so self-absorbed, but this week was different. He'd been working *SO* very hard to get to where he was, and this week seemed to show such grand promise for a brighter future. Not only was there potential for a promotion, but also a chance of reaching the next level in his relationship with his girlfriend Amber appeared to be very much on the horizon!

A nagging part at the back of Miles' mind told him that he should not have been so flippant to someone whom he had known, and supportively admired, for such a long time. Unfortunately, there were a number of security protocols in place, which disallowed him to be able to send or receive text messages until he logged his phone into the secure server at his desk. Having to wait until he got off of the elevator before he could know whether she had replied or not, was starting to eat at him, despite his jovial mood. The response finally came through. Taking a slow deep breath, he read the message, and a relieved smile crossed his face. Pondering for a moment, he nodded to himself, as he eyed the clock, and texted back,

"Yes, I will definitely be there!"

All was well between him and his dearest friend; she still wanted him to come over and help get some work done on the house. He had hoped, and possibly assumed, that she would understand how much respect and admiration he had for her. Realizing that Angelique's husband, Jack Erebus, was away on business, he knew that there was renovation work to be done, and she would not be able to handle it all on her own.

Upon returning to his desk, after having logged into the server, Miles discovered a new e-mail waiting in his inbox stating that his presence was being requested in Mr. Archos' office on Wednesday at 3:00pm. He glared determinedly at the computer screen, wrote a quick, but professional, acknowledgement in response:

"Thank you for providing me with this opportunity to meet with Mr. Archos. I am writing to confirm that I will be there promptly at 3pm on Wednesday."

Kyri Archos was the President of the company. Miles was feeling very confident about this e-mail and the pending meeting. He'd heard rumours of the company restructuring, opening up some positions, and he had been striving to progress in the company for a few years. However, he knew better than to allow himself get too distracted with thoughts of his, seemingly inevitable, promotion, and resumed working on the remaining tasks of the day.

☉☉☉

CENTRUS LABORATORIES:
EXPERIMENTAL SCIENCES DEPARTMENT
2:28pm, Tuesday October 21st, 2014

While events were looking set to fulfill the positive potential that Miles had attempted, in vain, to deny himself, developments elsewhere were also showing some kind of potential. Whether it was to be of a positive or negative variety, it was too soon to tell.

A dark cloaked figure pored over a Tele-visual display to analyze data on an experiment that was being put through a test phase. It had been years since a procedure of this sort had been attempted, or even approved for trial runs, and this time it was being kept very hush-hush.

The mysterious, slightly disfigured man, who was working alone in the large, dimly lit room, was pleased with the information that he was receiving. The weather factors, time, and location parameters all seemed ideal for the requirements of the project's anticipated successful outcome.

Just as it seemed that the test run of the experiment was going to work, and perhaps even improve upon the results of the original effort from so many years ago, the screen flashed a bright crimson red and a warning siren wailed. The test phase halted as the screen simply showed the same 2 words in an oscillating rainbow font:

★★★*QUANTUBUS EFFECT!!!*★★★

The cloaked figure slammed his fist down against the desk, a bit harder than he had intended to, denting the sheet metal platform in front of the display panel. He hissed and his cold, grey eyes absorbed & reflected the bright colours of the screen, focusing intently upon the repeated words. He knew immediately that these words had a very specific meaning, and that they threatened not only the future of the experiment, but could spell certain doom for the planet if the tested experiment were ever attempted in real-time conditions.

The multi-coloured glimmering words on the screen were almost taunting him as he growled at them in response. His cloaked form was visibly shaken with a frustrated rage.

"Not again!" He muttered, as he brought his hand over the crown of his head to finally protect his glowing, sensitive eyes from the brightness of the screen, making a vain effort to maintain control.

CHAPTER 2

STRUGGLING WITH THE INEVITABLE

Understandably, Miles felt the time leading up to the big meeting seemingly dragging along. He distracted himself with the enjoyment of quality time spent with his girlfriend Amber; they were ready to celebrate, albeit rather prematurely. Miles could scarcely contain his excitement regarding the pending meeting. Despite a restless Tuesday night, he awoke buzzing with energy and motivation. Wednesday morning came and went. Miles packed a lunch, staying at his desk in case the meeting time was suddenly changed.

By 3pm, Miles was on the 4th floor, waiting patiently for Mr. Archos to come out and greet him. 15 minutes later, Miles gazed at the wall clock intently, until he heard the large office door open. He didn't have to try very hard to force a confident smile across his lips as he arose to face his boss.

"Miles, please, please come in!" the shorter, heavy set man exclaimed. Miles entered nodding in respectful acknowledgement to Mr. Archos. "Please sit down, may I get you anything? Coffee? Tea?"

Not wanting to seem abrupt, impatient or rude; Miles paused and then politely declined; sitting in the very comfortable chair positioned in front of Mr. Archos' desk.

Mr. Archos, meanwhile, retrieved a file folder from his receptionist's desk and closed the door upon entering the office.

"I am very sorry to have kept you waiting; it's been one of those months."

"Oh, I understand, Sir", he blurted out too quickly, as he realized almost at once. He felt a little more uneasy now and didn't know why.

"I'm sure that you are aware of the changes in personnel that have been taking place over the past few weeks," Mr. Kyri Archos started, and laid the folder flat upon his desk.

Miles nodded silently; trying to hide the eagerness that he felt was shining through his baby blue eyes.

"The reason I've called you in here today", Mr. Archos continued, clearing his throat somewhat hesitantly. "Is to let you know that, as part of the budget cutbacks we are being forced to make, I'm afraid that we are going to have to terminate your employment with us, as of Friday afternoon, at four o'clock."

Miles almost bit his tongue, having anticipated an offer of promotion, only for the words that were spoken to be of a completely opposite nature. He found himself taken aback by a combination of shock, fury, disbelief, and anger.

Struggling to maintain his composure, he stammered, "Friday? **THIS** Friday?" He could sense that he was a bit physically shaken by the thought of ending such a positive month with unemployment.

"I tried my best to go to bat for you on this," Kyri responded sympathetically with a frown and a nod. "I fought every step of the way against the prospect of losing such a valued employee; which is why I can give you so little notice. But, what you have to understand is, the economy has hit us hard this year. The company is restructuring in order to survive. This was not an easy decision, but it was one that ultimately had to be made."

All Miles could think was: *"WHY ME?"*, but he kept that question to himself. Clearing his throat, not wanting to appear spiteful or unprofessional and risk ruining a potential reference, Miles arose from his seat.

"Thank you for taking the time to tell me in person, rather than over the phone or by e-mail", Miles replied, extending his hand.

Mr. Archos rose to his feet and shook the offered hand firmly.

"Best of luck to you, Mr. Militis," Mr. Archos was somewhat relieved with the level of composure he observed in Miles' reaction to this unfortunate news. "Please be sure to have your desk cleaned out by three-thirty on Friday, Human Resources will want you to fill out some paperwork before you leave."

Miles tried very hard to stifle a sigh of disappointment, nodding once more before turning away, and moving towards the door. The bounce in his step had faded. All of his efforts, his hard work and his dedication were about to amount to virtually nothing.

After returning to his desk, he packed up some of his things and left the office a bit early. His mind was reeling and it felt futile to focus on work.

☺☺☺

CENTRUS LABORATORIES: EXPERIMENTAL SCIENCES DEPARTMENT
4:04pm, Wednesday October 22nd, 2014

Focus was challenging for the cloaked figure in the top secret laboratory. He had been agonizing over the results of the failed test. Tormentingly, the sound of the alarm still rang in his ears. He had unplugged the Tele-visual display to keep it from reminding him exactly how the test had failed; and to prevent it from affecting his eyes.

Bowing his head even lower than before, the man looked ready to collapse, until a door on the far side of the room opened. The interruption caused the blaring noise that had once filled the room to cease, and prompted the figure to sit up straighter. The bright, outside light poured into the dimly lit room; causing its sole occupant to squeal and writhe in agony.

"My apologies, Lupo," the new arrival swiftly responded, and dimmed the light in the hallway. "What is your report?" the visitor enquired.

"You should know better than to interrupt and open the door to my lab unannounced," the cloaked recluse grumbled. Taking a moment to recover from the sudden shock of the bright illumination, his glowing eyes readjusting as the light was dimmed. With only the slightest hesitation, the cloaked man turned towards the silhouette standing in the doorway and reported:

"We are ready to begin!"

☺☺☺

MI POSTEVO TIPOTA INC.
Thursday October 23rd, 2014

It was the beginning of the end for Miles. During his last two days of work, he was unable to be as productive as was his standard. However, he still did his very best to not leave any assignments unfinished. He had just finished clearing his desk out, when a new text message arrived from Angelique.

"Are you and Amber still coming tonight for our monthly gathering and game night?" These words appeared on Miles' phone and it caused him to frown. He hadn't yet had the heart to tell his best friend about being laid off.

"Is it alright if I come over earlier?" he wrote back, biting his lip to stop from breaking into tears. After a brief pause, the response appeared.

"Yes, certainly...I can just make more spaghetti. Cooking it for one is never fun or easy anyway."

While heading to the Human Resources department, Miles looked at the text and allowed himself a little smile, before slipping the phone into his pocket. Approaching the door, he could feel his smile slipping away, as he entered the office where he would surrender his badge and his subsequent interest in a company that had been such an integral part of his identity for so many years.

With the papers signed, Miles sighed, taking one longing last look around. He tightly gripped the handle of his briefcase as he turned to walk towards the exit. He said his final goodbyes before closing the door behind him.

He descended the steps into the subway station, and down onto the platform; going through the usual motions that he could almost do in his sleep. He quickly realized that he might have been better off getting released earlier in the week, rather than facing this Friday evening rush hour crunch one more time. He watched the nearby screen as the news of recent crimes, scandals, protest marches, and riots appeared. He then caught a glimpse of the forecast calling for the violently windy rain storm that was expected to hit on Saturday afternoon. Shaking his head as the train arrived; he moved to join the soon-to-be human sardines crammed into the subway car. The doors closed swiftly behind him, cutting out the still ever-growing mob of impatient commuters on the platform, who would have to await the next train.

He stood, holding a pole for most of the trip. He kept his eyes shut, as he desperately tried to contain his emotions. The noise, the smell, the feeling of being pressed up against so many bodies at once; it was more than he could bear sometimes; even when he wasn't coping with emotional turmoil.

Having finally arrived at his apartment, Miles dropped his case to the floor by the door, resisting the urge to kick it across the room. He took off his work clothes, and tried to refresh himself with a nice hot shower; getting cleaned up to meet his best friend for, what would likely be, a night of great food and plenty of extremely welcome wine.

THE EREBUS RESIDENCE
8:08pm, Friday October 24th, 2014

With Friday rush hour crowds, ridiculous transit delays and other factors; Miles arrived at Angelique's house an hour later than he'd anticipated. The home was quite beautiful, with a well-groomed and landscaped yard; though some parts of the house itself *clearly* showed signs of needing repair. Angelique's husband, Jack Erebus, would normally have been present and very capable of handling the renovations and other work on his house; but he was filming on a location in Europe. Miles had recalled discussing the film with Jack, and was fascinated with the idea of a film that had to do with Ancient Greece & Greek Philosophers, and their impact on the development of the world & society.

As he surveyed the foundation, evaluating some of its specific needs, he just missed the glimmer of a faint glow shining from a hole in the wall. He nodded to himself as he approached the front door, *"Some good hard manual labour might be just what the Doctor ordered to help me deal with all that I'm going through right now,"* he thought.

At the sound of the door chime, the door opened to reveal a statuesque, blonde-haired, young lady who smiled brightly at her dear friend.

"I wasn't sure if you were going to make it, Miles!" Angelique greeted him. She stepped back, inviting him to enter. "But when I didn't get a response to my last 2 texts, I figured that you were probably just stuck on the subway; and I adjusted my cooking schedule a bit, just in case."

With a sigh, Miles nodded in acknowledgement. "It's definitely not getting any better out there," he replied, a part of him momentarily musing over the scientific stuff that she'd said earlier she wanted to discuss with him.

"How's Amber doing?" Angelique asked as she strode towards the kitchen. "I'm surprised you didn't bring her with you." She stirred the pasta, seemingly unaware of the pain that Miles hid. She assumed that he was frustrated by the extended trip at the end of a long, stressful week.

"She's not coming, we…we sorta broke up", Miles replied, which was quickly followed by the loud clang of a ladle dropping against a pot. Angelique rushed back out to the hallway and gave her friend a comforting hug. He allowed himself to melt into her soothing embrace before continuing, "There's more, but it can wait till after dinner. I certainly am hungry!"

Angelique squeezed a bit harder, rubbing Miles' back, and then stepped back.

"Dinner's almost ready. Why don't you go into the wine cellar and pick something appropriate?" She beamed, knowing his penchant for selecting the right wine for any given occasion.

Miles hesitated, then smiled and turned excitedly towards the door that led to the wine cellar. He was VERY familiar with the majority of their selection and knew exactly what to choose! Having found the fine Argentina Malbec that he was looking for, Miles returned to the hallway. Upon entering the kitchen, he was quickly met with the aroma of the dinner being prepared.

"Do I detect a hint of mushrooms in the sauce?" he asked as he reached for 2 wine glasses.

"Yes, indeed!" Angelique smiled at him, responding excitedly, "my own special blend." She tried to stop herself from shaking her head at the thought of Amber leaving a great guy like Miles.

He licked his lips a little as he exited towards the dining room; setting out the glasses, and opening the wine bottle. The food was served moments later. Jack was lucky to have found Angelique. In addition to her other talents, she kept their home organized and cooked with flair and passion, The spaghetti dinner was the best that he had tasted in years, and to his own credit, the wine was the perfect complement to the meal.

Over the 2-3 hours that followed, Miles revealed to Angelique how he had gotten laid off from work, and how Amber had chosen that moment to leave him as a result. They opened and polished off a second bottle of wine before they finished the discussion.

"Since you're coming back tomorrow to help with the house, why don't you stay over in the spare room in the basement?" Angelique suggested.

"Thanks," Miles said. The bedroom was right next to the wine cellar, and the bed was particularly cozy. He had stayed over in that room many times before; sometimes when he was house sitting, other times when he was just spending a weekend with Angelique and Jack.

"I hope you don't mind but there are a couple of other outdoor chores I need your help with, as well as the ones we talked about," she said.

"No problem," he replied, and headed toward the basement, to that remarkably comfy bed. Its mattress had helped him to drift effortlessly to sleep, unlike his experiences with other mattresses.

And the guest room was reasonably habitable, in spite of being in the midst of its own repairs and renovations.

Miles laid his briefcase gently upon the bedside table, and changed for bed. Looking around the room, he sat down on the edge of the bed and sighed contentedly. Whatever had happened this week, he was ending it on a positive note, in the comfort of a bed that was sure to join the wine in lulling him into a deep and restful sleep.

CHAPTER 3

THE STORM

THE EREBUS RESIDENCE
7:30am, Saturday October 25th, 2014

It was a windy, rainy morning. Miles awoke from a somewhat restful slumber. His alarm woke him in time to arise and face the day, and the work he'd promised to do. Having showered and dressed, he grabbed his laptop and went upstairs to the main floor. The weather was as horrible as the forecast had promised. He'd hoped to avoid it. Though spending the night wasn't his original plan, it ended up working out in the end as the wind storm had struck early!

"Damn inaccurate weathermen!" he muttered to himself. He gazed out of the window at the unfriendly, cold, bitter weather, with powerful winds blowing at 35-40km/h and gusts blowing beyond 50km/h. It was the kind of weather that he would often try to work his schedule around; and many others would likely do the same. As it was late October, the wind was blowing the remaining leaves from the trees with a violent ferocity.

At breakfast, he and Angelique agreed to postpone the additional outdoor tasks for the day, because of the storm. The rain would've damaged some of the materials that he was supposed to help retrieve for her. He was relieved, but also found that he was still quite tired; despite the amazingly restful sleep that his favourite guest bed had provided him. *"This damn weather is likely impacting negatively upon my energy level too"*, he thought. Days like this made him dream of the day when the invention of weather control technology would finally be realized.

Despite his nagging fatigue, and perhaps against his own better judgement, he opted to browse the internet to catch up on email, social media, and news updates. He had grown tired and frustrated over the number of news stories about car thefts, energy conservation-related crises, and people crying foul over rights, equality and alleged "inappropriate" material found in the media. More often than not, he knew that he was either going to find bad news or stories that probably should never have been published in the first place (a.k.a. "slow news day").

To cap it off, he noticed a story that *really* did not help his mood or his frame of mind. *"More foolishness,"* he thought, shaking his head indignantly.

Angelique frowned, while watching her friend struggling to come to terms with the events of the morning. Accepting that there was little she could do to help him; she gently patted him on the back as she proceeded to the second floor to take a shower and get ready for the day ahead.

Miles had developed a strong dislike for the ways in which the world around him was changing; but he had come to terms with the fact that there was little he could really do about it. The more news of the morning that he read, the more he wanted to throw his fragile old laptop computer across the room, out of frustration.

The fact that it was one that he had occasionally used for the job he no longer had, only served to remind him of his recent failures.

Taking a slow deep breath, he chose instead to simply close the computer and walk away from it. Having left a brief text for Angelique, indicating that he was going to get more sleep, he returned to his "borrowed" bedroom, and sat upon the edge of the bed. Having realized that he hadn't yet torn the next page from his "This Day in History" calendar, he proceeded to do so. The page for October 25th was unexpectedly noteworthy, laying out several historical facts that captured Miles' interest.

1492: Christopher Columbus' flagship the Santa
        Maria lands at Dominican Republic.
1861: Toronto Stock Exchange created.
1870: Postcards first used in USA.
1881: Pablo Picasso was born.
1930: First scheduled transcontinental air service
        began.
1955: Tappan sells first microwave oven.

Miles had recently developed a fascination with learning about when things happened, when new technologies were brought forth, new discoveries, etc. As the storm continued outside, he could feel his fatigue weigh more heavily upon him. Laying back on the bed, he stared at the ceiling. His mind spun imagining all of the things that had gone wrong, but could have been so much better, if only... if only...

The wind howled and rattled the windows which, in turn, shook some of the partly exposed wall panels in Miles' room. The renovations were incomplete, but still solid enough to be considered reasonably "cozy". In spite of his thoughts going into overdrive, he felt himself drifting into a very relaxed state...

this mattress had that effect on him. He was glad Angelique had kept it during the summer clean-out preceding the repairs and renovations taking place. This incredible bed accomplished something that not even hypnosis could manage; it set Miles' body at ease. His tense shoulders and neck seemed to loosen completely in mere moments. Morpheus had set upon him in no time. The violence of the storm became a faded, distant memory. He could rest now, uninterrupted by phone calls or alarms, and likely awaken quite refreshed.

🕐🕑🕒

CENTRUS LABORATORIES: RESEARCH LAB #2
9:06am, Saturday October 25th, 2014

In a remote top-secret facility, located beneath the base of the CN Tower, a bearded, middle-aged Caucasian gentleman peered over the shoulder of a younger Asian scientist. In front of them, monitors and scanners recorded a number of results from the complex experiment they were running. The bearded man's eyes glistened as the information being presented indicated that his grand plan was closer to reaching fruition.

"Good, Professor, EXCELLENT!" the gentleman uttered, a strong British accent was noticeable in his voice. "I've waited a long time to see results like this from our efforts. This will be the greatest accomplishment ever made here at Centrus Laboratories! Dinner is on me!"

Doctor Roger Thascalos had been working at Centrus Laboratories for the better part of 20 years, and had hoped that some positive results from the current experiment would allow him a greater level of prestige than he'd already earned during that time. His younger assistant, an Asian professor by the name of Eric Nidell, was working under Dr. Thascalos as an apprentice.

Eric Nidell, smiled slightly, but he felt there was still something a bit off about the data being received. "Doctor Thascalos, I'm not so sure that we have achieved complete success. But, once I've verified the stability of the data, I'll take you up on the offer. I think we both could certainly use a break…"

As if on cue, the moment of potential celebration was interrupted by a klaxon sounding loudly in a different part of the room. Startled by the relentless cacophony of whines and groans emanating from a secondary control terminal, both men became aware of a dangerous instability that had not been foreseen nor prepared for. Turning instinctively towards his own screen, the young apprentice read the preliminary information that rapidly began to appear. Having then raced to a central computer interface, he began working his fingers vigorously over the keyboard in an attempt to further diagnose the problem, and its impact on their experimental efforts. The alarm stopped sounding moments before the updated information scrolled across the monitor.

The two men exchanged a glance of concerned astonishment. The older gentleman groaned, addressing his younger associate,

"Whatever you do, Eric, please don't say "I told you so."" They then both returned their attention to the data they'd just received.

One thing was glaringly apparent; the celebratory dinner would clearly have to wait…

☺☺☺

THE EREBUS RESIDENCE
12:21pm, Saturday October 25th, 2014

Angelique, having received the text Miles had left for her, called down to him for lunch; but got no reply. She descended the staircase towards the guest bedroom. When she entered the room, after having knocked and received no response, she discovered that the bed was unmade, Miles' briefcase was still in the room… but Miles was gone!

CHAPTER 4

ODD AWAKENING

Miles awoke from his deep sleep to discover that he was not where he had originally dozed off. He rolled from his left side onto his back. Even the surface that he was laying on was not the same. He tried to open his eyes only to be blinded by an intense light that caused them to immediately squeeze shut. He winced, his left hand and arm extended instinctively to protect him from the brightness, and almost immediately the light dimmed slightly. He slowly opened his eyes again to find that the light source was not like anything he'd ever seen before. It had automatically reacted to his hand, and reduced the intensity of its illumination.

Regaining his senses and clarity of vision, Miles sat up and spun his legs towards the floor. He discovered that he was resting on a floating cot of sorts. Pale, plain-looking walls surrounded his bed on 3 sides. The fourth side of the large rectangular room had what looked like a door.

"Good morning!" a voice abruptly crackled from a speaker near the far wall. The noise echoed throughout the practically empty room, and Miles winced again, nearly falling back onto the bed. He waved his hand in a downwards motion, towards the direction of the speakers.

"My apologies," the voice replied. The volume from the speaker had diminished with the same apparently automated response as the lights to his hand gesture. But where was he? The voice interrupted his curiosity before he could ask. "Unfortunately, you are not a known citizen of our community, and we were unable to induce your consciousness. This prohibited us from being able to adapt your surroundings to the sensitivity of your ocular and auditory receptors."

Miles nodded slowly to indicate his understanding, but groaned and shook his head slightly; bewildered and brimming with questions..

"If you are hungry, please feel free to approach the forest green panel on the wall to your right. We will talk soon. No doubt you have many questions; as we, naturally, have for you as well."

"I don't recognize that voice," he thought to himself. But then, why would he? The person who spoke to him indicated that he had somehow arrived in a community where *he* was unfamiliar to *them!* Taking a slow deep breath, he pressed himself up and off of the floating cot. A few moments later, it gradually lowered itself into a moulded space in the floor, and seemed to disappear. Miles turned back to watch it, shaking his head as he struggled to process all that he had experienced in the last five minutes. Turning to the wall where he was directed to find food, he approached the green panel. The wall surrounding it seemed to be constructed of a material that he had not seen before...particularly not for a wall.

His stomach rumbled. "Food..." he softly whispered, wondering what he could want, and then he mulled over what he could handle. He had to force himself to think about getting some nourishment before he could satisfy his troubled curiosity. He recalled the wonderful breakfast that he had enjoyed with Angelique whilst hearing the incredible storm on that otherwise drab morning. It seemed so long ago. Thoughts of how his morning had begun, only served to raise new concerns regarding what might've happened to Angelique?

Pressing his right index and middle finger against the green panel, he heard it groan momentarily and then become transparent, as a part of the panelling slid away. Left in front of him was the refreshingly familiar sight and smell of bacon and eggs, with a fresh cup of French Vanilla coffee.

"Perfect!" he almost shouted aloud. But that's when it occurred to him, that it was indeed *exactly* what he was thinking of; from the last meal that he recalled having eaten. While hesitant at first, he reached into the open compartment, and grabbed the tray holding his food. Turning, he looked around sheepishly, and with a slight hint of befuddled embarrassment, as there was nowhere for him to sit and enjoy his meal.

"Allow me!" That same voice crackled from the speaker. A comfortable-looking folding chair and small table materialized a few feet in front of him; much to Miles' amazement. Wherever he was, it almost didn't even *feel* like Earth! He approached the table and sat upon the chair, which seemed to adjust its cushioning and comfort level to his weight and body type. An eerie feeling to experience for the first time, to say the least!

☺☺☺

CENTRUS LABORATORIES:
RESEARCH LAB #2
3:00pm, Saturday October 25th, 2014

"But that's impossible!" exclaimed the bearded Dr. Thascalos, gaping in astonishment at the screen. "There was nothing in the plan specifications, nor in our projection studies, that could have even come close to creating that kind of anomaly!"

Professor Nidell spun around on his chair to face his partner.

"Regardless of what we thought would or might potentially happen," the younger man started. "It DOES seem unlikely that the system would be registering an event that did not or could not occur." He returned his attention to the screen, and began typing away at the keyboard again to acquire more details regarding the incident. "A more important consideration to examine may be with regards to what we can do about it, now that it HAS happened."

The lead scientist nodded without much enthusiasm, irritated by the emotionless analysis that his Asian assistant was practically famous for.

"Yes, I suppose you are right. I thought we'd finally seen the light at the end of this particularly arduous tunnel, but I didn't expect the light to be a red one!" The elder gentleman's face drooped, his eyes bugging out from a further revelation.

This sudden outcome would further impact the original experiment that they had felt so close to successfully completing.

When he had almost completely finished eating everything on his breakfast tray, Miles heard the voice erupt from the speakers once again; the volume was still lower than the first time.

"When you have finished your food, and feel ready to talk, please come towards this video screen by the door and press the small blue button next to it. An attendant will be with you shortly, and will guide you to the appropriate room."

Taking one last sip of his very satisfying French Vanilla-flavoured coffee, he nodded slowly. Pushing up from his comfortable chair, he determinedly headed towards the door, and pressed the blue button. While he waited, his gaze was drawn towards the blue button; he was convinced that it was not there when he first looked around; nor, come to think of it, was there a forest green panel! Before he could ponder the implications of these inconsistencies, the large door in front of him clicked and hummed, sliding to the left. A sophisticated looking robot appeared on the outside, and glided in to greet Miles.

"Greetings, honoured guest, we hope that you have enjoyed your meal. I am Attendant Bot IDL-21; please follow me to the meeting room." The robot was quite tall and slender, with a mix of a platinum silver and a stone grey colouring covering much of its form. It gestured towards the hall with a simple metallic hand, then turned and started to lead the way.

Despite being met with this new and friendly, yet unfamiliar technology, Miles didn't hesitate for a moment; he was determined to learn where he was and how he got there.

CHAPTER 5

THE PROFESSOR

Miles had no reason to doubt the robot's intentions, and he knew that he wanted answers that only the people expecting him at this meeting area should be able to provide to him. He followed a few feet behind the robot into a long corridor, as the large door behind him automatically slid shut, locked, and disappeared into the surrounding wall. Following the robot a short distance further led them to another rather large door that hummed, then clicked, and slid open. He followed his guide into the room, and watched as the lighting within adjusted slightly, much like the other light source had done shortly after he awoke.

"Attendant Bot IDL-21, completing the assigned task. Allow me to introduce..." the robot paused.

"Miles...Miles Militis!" Miles spoke right up instinctively. Quickly realizing what he'd done, he narrowed his gaze at the Attendant Bot. Thinking to himself about how clever the metal man was to indirectly prompt him to reveal his identity so effortlessly.

A tall, elderly man stood in the centre of the room. Having discarded his white lab coat to reveal a finely tailored burgundy suit underneath, he handed the coat to IDL-21. The Attendant Bot took the lab coat, and swiftly exited the room; the door automatically closing behind him. The well-dressed man watched on as the robot exited with the lab coat, which wasn't quite what he wanted. He frowned as the door slid shut behind the mechanical man, but then tried to force a smile as he gestured towards Miles.

"Please, come and sit down. You'll have to excuse IDL-21, he's had a few bugs in his system lately that apparently have not all been worked out" And, with a wave of his hand, a soft leather recliner materialized opposite a folding chair, similar to the one Miles had sat upon while eating his meal.

Miles gave an appreciative nod of acknowledgement and sat upon the recliner, as it seemed to be the chair that was being offered to him. The older man sat in the folding chair opposite and looked Miles over carefully and curiously.

"We were not able to find any means of identification in your pockets, nor were our DNA scanners able to locate a match in our Hall of Records. You are quite the enigma, Mr. Militis." A coughing fit interrupts the host's introduction. Clearing his throat, he continued, "Excuse me, my name is Archaios, Professor Olim Archaios. It is a unique privilege for a man of my advanced years to sit face to face with, what could be, a final opportunity to be able to prove himself."

Miles widened his gaze, his original astonishment at the similarity between this old gentleman's name and that of his former employer was swiftly brushed aside as he felt incredibly confused but, at the same time, concerned.

"I'm not sure I understand what you mean, Professor."

Professor Archaios stared intently at his guest and then nodded slowly. "I had a feeling that you might ask. I'm not sure how things work, wherever it is that you come from, but this community... this world, in fact, has its own special set of guidelines in place. Through the guidance of logicians and visionaries, politicians and clerics; we have managed to narrowly avoid overpopulating the planet needlessly by assigning a mortal age limit of 100 years. On the approach of this time of life, a person wishing to exceed this limit is obligated to provide proof of a significant contribution towards society, their respective community or the world as a whole. Otherwise, they would be required, by law, to submit to a death of their own choosing, on their 100th birthday."

Miles leaned far aback in his chair; the soothing comfort of the leather became quite ineffective; the sheer horror of what he had just heard was almost too much for him to contemplate. His mind, once again, struggled to think of possible answers to the questions that filled his head. He could not hide his revulsion for the way this society opted to control its population, despite the fact that overcrowding was all too real a problem in the world that he knew.

"I see that it is not the same where you come from." The Professor nodded once again. "It is a way of life that the vast majority of us have learned to accept, and we educate our young about these tenets."

"Vast majority," Miles thought, which led him to assume that there was still an element in this...this...retardation of a society that chose to fight for the right to live beyond 100. This consideration only prompted a further curiosity, *"Could these people really live past 100? Did so many people really even reach 100?"* He realized that he would probably have to try to find answers from elsewhere.

"So, you are saying that you and the others in this society have somehow managed to prolong your existence up to the age of 100 with the potential for living beyond?" Miles finally spoke up, trying to remain calm and confident in his tone and approach.

With a twinkle appearing in his eye and a smile forming across his lips at the query, the Professor nodded.

"A great many can and do live long healthy lives," Olim replied, with a sense of pride and accomplishment. "It was an inevitable result of the creative advances of medical sciences and research, plus the seemingly endless development of new technologies. I won't bore you with the details."

Miles couldn't believe his ears! Where had he found himself? Was he having an incredibly vivid dream? Everything from the food, to the feel of the wall panels to the cot that he awoke upon, and the furniture that he sat on strongly conflicted with the thought that he might be dreaming. It was all simply *too* real not to be…well, *real*! He rationalized the unlikelihood of it all being some kind of dream by reminding himself that, while he'd wished for things to be different in his world, he did not have a vivid enough imagination to pull together all of this detail into such a tangible realm.

"You said the "vast majority" of the population had accepted this 100 year age restriction." He started to reference more of what the Professor had told him, in order to further his own understanding. "I'm assuming this means that there are those who try to work around it?"

A frown briefly replaced the proud smile that had formed across the Professor's lips.

"Yes, unfortunately, there ARE some heretics among us." Archaios' voice had a strong hint of bitterness to it now. "Criminals who choose to rebel against our established way of life. I am uncertain whether they are insane, uneducated or merely afraid. It's not really a strict limitation, however. As I said, if a significant accomplishment or contribution has been made on the person's behalf, he or she will not be expected to end their lives prematurely nor so abruptly."

Frustration within Miles was starting to mount and it showed, as he fired his next question out with repugnance.

"And who gets to determine what contributions or accomplishments are significant?"

Archaios sighed, shaking his head once again.

"You are far too young to have to worry about details regarding that. It is more important for you to know that you are safe, respected and will be well-treated as an honoured guest in this Complex." The Professor was interrupted by a signal beeping from his pocket, which he quickly deactivated. "I'm afraid I do not have time to answer more of your questions right now. However, you are more than welcome to explore on your own. The Guest Quarters in which you regained consciousness will remain available for you to return to, should you wish to use it to sleep, eat or relax."

Before the Professor could get up to leave, Miles arose from his recliner and stepped into his host's path.

"I just have 2 more questions for you, Professor." Miles spoke a bit faster, "You referred to this place as a Complex, what is it called?"

Olim Archaios, in spite of being a bit perturbed by the suddenness of his guest's actions, understood his guest's need and thirst for knowledge.

"I prefer to just call it the Complex," Professor Archaios replied, with a fatigued sigh. "But officially it is named the Scientific Unity Complex." The look on his face remaining impassive after answering this question, knowing his guest was not yet aware of the irony behind the name.

"Okay, that should be an easy enough name to remember while I am out exploring." Miles started again, oblivious to the suspiciously vacant look on the Professor's face. "And lastly, I know this is going to sound a bit unusual, perhaps crazy, but there's something that I desperately need to know in order to explore the area outside with any semblance of safety and comfort." He hesitated a moment, perhaps it was his uneasiness that made him unaware of his host's reaction to his previous query. "This place it....well, it *IS* Earth, isn't it?"

"Oh yes, this is Earth alright." Professor Archaios confirmed, his face giving off a quizzical expression to the question that was just asked. Looking Miles over once more, the Professor pursed his lips thoughtfully. "You may wish to return to the room we have given you first. Some clothing will be made available. This will allow you to explore without arousing unnecessary attention, concern or fear; and should allow you to feel more comfortable during your journey."

"Thank you, Professor," Miles said as he stepped aside to allow him to exit. Since he was still uncertain about how the doors worked, he followed quickly after Professor Archaios, before heading back towards his room as the Professor disappeared around a corner.

The older gentleman waited until his strange young guest was well out of sight and earshot, and then proceeded to press his palm against a, barely visible, scanner next to a concealed door, which bleeped and blooped before the door slid open, and Olim Archaios stepped inside.

CHAPTER 6

PREPARING FOR THE UNKNOWN

SCIENTIFIC UNITY COMPLEX:
GUEST QUARTERS

As he returned to his assigned room, Miles managed to figure out how to activate the door mechanism to trigger it to open, and stepped in. Looking around somewhat sheepishly, he noticed a glowing screen on the wall opposite the one that the food had come out of. Approaching the screen, he was greeted warmly by a text message:

> *Welcome, Citizen!*
> *Please press the image on the screen that depicts the style of clothing that you are looking for.*

Scanning the array of icons, he pondered how best to introduce himself to this strange new world. He spotted a separate row of buttons along the right side of the screen. One of them read "Voice". He pressed it gently, and a female voice spoke, with the same level of volume that the Professor had adjusted the observation window speaker to.

"Greetings, Citizen, how may I help you today?"

Basking in the soft sound of the automated voice, he noticed how friendly everything and everyone seemed to be. *"If this is Earth, why is it so different? What's changed?"* he wondered. He then turned his thoughts towards Angelique, imagining what might've happened to her and what she must be thinking if he really did just disappear from the guest bedroom in the midst of that violent wind storm? Realizing that he needed to concentrate on the matters at hand, he replied to the question.

"I would like some casual attire that would befit a man my age in this time period," Miles said, biting his bottom lip, realizing he sounded more like an automaton than the automated voice did! Maybe he'd picked up that speech pattern from the Attendant or the Professor?

The screen and the large panel that appeared beside it throbbed and groaned. The wall panel slid open to reveal a wardrobe of varying colours, but very similar designs. He chose carefully from the provided selection and stepped back from the wall. A mirror materialized on the wall next to the closet containing the wardrobe, allowing Miles to observe his appearance in the new clothing.

The voice spoke again, "We hope that those clothes will help you to feel comfortable as you adjust to your new environment. Is there anything else that we can provide for you?"

That seemingly altruistic desire to accommodate could not escape his attention. Thinking carefully about his journey ahead, he realized that he didn't even know where he was!

"Oh! A ummm...a map? Could I have a map of the local area?"

A humming sound briefly filled the room, and the voice spoke once more:

"You will find a portable computer, with a detailed interactive map, on the bed. Should you have any further questions or requirements, please do not hesitate to press the "Voice" button again. Happy travels!" The glow of the screen faded to match the textured blankness of the surrounding wall.

☺☺☺

QUANTUS ENTERPRISES:
SCIENCE & TECHNOLOGY DEPARTMENT

Meanwhile, in a luxuriously ornate, symmetrical, and unique-looking structure, located in the centre of a vast collection of smaller buildings and depots, the arrival of Miles Militis was not only noticed, but a cause for great concern.

A young, red-haired & pale skinned young lady by the name of Anita O'Dell was finding her way around the building, familiarizing herself with the layout, when she espied a man she only knew as "The Administrator" looking rather concerned at a computer screen in a small tracking room. Not wishing to interrupt his concentration, and make a poor impression during her first week on the job, she stepped in quietly to more closely observe what he was reacting to. She watched as his forehead wrinkled and his eyes narrowed, indicating to her a mix of frustration and possibly disbelief at what he was reading.

"Excuse me, Administrator," she started, finally letting her curiosity get the better of her; announcing her presence to the oblivious man rather abruptly as she approached the computer terminal to get a closer look.

"I take it that there be more to this information on the screen, and that it be bad news?" Anita continued; her jade-green eyes glistening in the well-lit room. She frowned slightly as she was unaware of a connection between this report and any prior events; nor was she conscious of any relevant factors in the information provided. She'd normally be excited by the prospect of something new and different occurring, particularly during her first week on the job; but the Administrator's reaction to the results of his research caused her to be more concerned and disappointed than positive.

The Administrator turned sharply, startled by the sound of another voice in the room. Recognizing the newest staff member of Quantus' Science and Technology department, he managed to form a half smile, but then frowned with a heavy sigh.

"The information on that screen is incomplete, worrisome, and yet, somehow so familiar..." he replied, gesturing to the terminal in an agitated manner. "It just doesn't make any logical sense; usually the computers in this room are completely inactive!"

Administrator Anthony Thascalos was a middle-aged scientist who was a bit on the short and slim side, clean shaven, with jet black hair. He had been project leader at Quantus Enterprises for over 15 years. His attention was redirected towards the computer terminal as it bleeped to indicate that more data was forthcoming. He pored over the new facts; his look of frustrated concern did not change. The newly added points on the computer monitor only served to confirm his suspicions. He finally turned away from the screen, his eyes closed slowly as his head tilted back. With a frown, he focused a narrow gaze in the direction of the domed ceiling.

"Not again!" he muttered with a disappointed sigh.

☺☺☺

SCIENTIFIC UNITY COMPLEX: GUEST QUARTERS

While looking at his new outfit in the mirror, Miles realized that there was one more thing that he needed to ask the friendly computer which had provided him access to his "more suitable" attire. Pressing the Voice button, he asked, "What's the weather going to be like outside of the Complex?"

"The Weather Control Station has promised those living in this region sunny skies and temperatures ranging between 25 and 30 degrees Celsius." The automated voice reported, "However, a brief thunderstorm is expected to begin in 2 hours, 17 minutes."

"*A weather control station?*" Miles asked himself, clearing his throat to avoid asking openly, but then cleared his throat. "Thank you, that will be all for now." The closet door slid shut, and the mirror disappeared into the wall. He turned towards the cot and saw the small computer lying on top of the neatly made bed. Grabbing the tablet, he tucked it under his arm, took a slow deep breath, and moved towards the door.

"Now to find the way out," he told himself, all the time plagued by some fundamental questions: Where was he? How did he come to be here? Why was everything so different? What other changes and differences would he come across, compared to the Earth that he knew? What challenges or perils lay beyond the safety of the Complex?

With electronic map in hand, he moved towards the door leading to the hallway, determined to find the exit. As if the Complex had, once again, read his mind; Miles *observed* a stream of rainbow coloured lights cascading along the wall, indicating the direction he should follow towards the exit. The Complex itself was aiding him in finding his way towards the well-labelled exit. The door slid open, allowing him to step through to the outside world.

☺☺☺

SCIENTIFIC UNITY COMPLEX: SECURITY CHAMBER K-1

Professor Olim Archaios observed the departure of his new honoured guest on the security monitor.

"He seems quite unaware of how he came to be here." The Professor reported into a communications device that was affixed to the security system. "I will continue to see if we can learn anything about him from his DNA, and recommend that the progress of his explorations be carefully observed by other means."

CHAPTER 7

CEASELESS WONDERS

It didn't take long for Miles to learn that the automated weather report was correct. The sun was shining brightly, and the sky was a stunning shade of blue. Miles inspected his new surroundings. The air, the street noise, even the ground beneath his feet all seemed somehow different from what he once knew. He began walking north along the road.

The vehicles that passed him hummed quietly, and appeared to hover about a foot above the roadway, which impressed him greatly. However, there was something else...something that didn't quite look right. *"THE CARS...they have no door locks!!!"* Miles struggled to stop himself from exclaiming the discovery aloud; not wishing to draw unnecessary or unusual attention; the idea that he had arrived in a world where car doors did not require locks was far more foreign to him than the advent of floating cars. He was also astonished to notice that there were several vehicles which sported, what appeared to be, company logos on them... often 2 or 3 different ones on each vehicle. *"There are too many of them for it to be some kind of convention, or a gathering of race car enthusiasts."* He thought.

Stopping a moment to look up into the sky, to admire just

how lovely a shade of blue it was, he watched as a shimmering ripple of purple light cascaded over the horizon. Startled by what he had seen, and the uncertainty of what it meant, he gaped at the otherwise clear blue sky as a few clouds gradually floated into view. Nobody else seemed to notice what he saw, which caused him to wonder whether he had imagined it?

Moments later, a blimp-like vehicle slowly drifted across the area of the sky that Miles was already fixated upon. The name "Quantus Enterprises" brightly shone from the slowly scrolling marquee lighting around its bulbous outer shell.

He was in absolute awe of where he had found himself, as he continued along the street. Passing pedestrians would greet him kindly, and he made certain to return the favour. Miles could not get over the fact that everyone was so very friendly, and that everything around him was so…clean!

☺☺☺

QUANTUS ENTERPRISES:
LOBOS CHAMBER #314

Unbeknownst to Miles, a security drone was discreetly hovering above and behind him. The design and markings did not match that of anything else in the area and yet, it managed to remain unnoticed, for the most part.

Surveillance screens flashed and flickered on a large console in a dark room. Observing the curious gentleman on the larger screen carefully, a shrouded figure reached a cybernetic hand forward to activate a switch. The console made a few grinding noises before hissing and finishing with a beep; producing statistical data on the contents being presented on the video screens. The figure checked and double-checked the information, as there seemed to be no discernible details on the figure that was approaching the main, central intersection of the downtown core.

The figure paused and leaned in closer to the monitor, adjusting the view to zoom in on the stranger.

"I don't believe it. It's not possible. It can't be…" the shrouded man growled speculatively, "It *COULD* be!!!"

Reaching his metallic exo-skeletal hand towards a different console, the mysterious figure quickly reprogrammed his drone to maintain discreet vigilance of the mysterious man, hoping to determine the identity and confirm if it was who he thought it was.

Miles had stopped at the street corner of what seemed to be a very busy intersection; but there were no street lights affixed to any of the lamp posts. There were visible panels making up the surface of the road, and the panels nearest the corner, on each side, were either glowing red or green from a light that shone from above the space. After the red light signalled the traffic coming to a stop, a coloured path lay before him which led to a large building across the way. It was most certainly the tallest building in the visible area. The powerfully imposing sign on the front of the building read "**MAIN LIBRARY**".

"*A library…*" Miles thought to himself. A hint of excitement sparked as he realized that, if there were answers to be had, he'd more than likely find them there. "*So, this city appreciated the accumulation of knowledge, to the extent that the largest building to be constructed in a given area was the one designed to store, maintain, and provide all of that information!*" Miles concluded proudly.

He crossed the street to the front doors of the Library, which slid open effortlessly and without hesitation as he approached. The surveillance drone quietly followed him towards the building, but remained hovering outside.

In the alcove between the double set of main doors, Miles admired the polished and well-designed surroundings. He stepped through the inner doors, and found himself facing a pair of elevators. A panel on the wall between them lit up moments after he entered the area.

Welcome to the Amgine City Main Library, Citizen!

What can I help you find today?

Miles wished he could meet the designers of the interface for the computer terminals that he'd encountered thus far; as his intrigue into its design and history was prevalent. But, he was in doubt that such a meeting would be possible. He observed the same "Voice" button on the right-hand side of the panel, and pressed it.

"Welcome, Citizen, we hope you are having an enjoyable afternoon. What can we help you find today?"

This voice was very different from the one he'd heard at the Scientific Unity Complex, this one was more gender-neutral. Miles tried to think of where it would be best for him to begin his quest for knowledge.

"Good afternoon," Miles replied. "I'm from out of town, and I'd like to learn about where I am, and perhaps read up on current events."

The panel dimmed slightly, groaning softly to process the request then the friendly voice responded, "Please proceed to the 4th Floor, where both the General Knowledge and Current Events departments can be found. General Knowledge can be accessed in sections 4190 through to 4440. Current Events information can be found in sections 4800 through 4999."

Miles was astounded, wondering *"for so many sections on a single floor…how could it be possible?"*

"Thank you" he said, nodding at the panel and entering the elevator as the doors slid open for him. The elevator didn't feel like it was moving at all, but he saw the number on the screen climb rather swiftly from 1 to 4. A bell sounded softly to indicate that he had arrived. As he stepped out of the elevator, he felt ever-more bewildered at where he had found himself. The lighting in the room was a soft green, in most areas. There were no actual books, per se, but individual kiosks and stations that were organized by department and section. This greatly helped improve his understanding of how there were so many sections on one floor, as the computer had described.

Miles approached an empty kiosk in the General Knowledge Department, carefully reaching for the glass door, only for it to automatically slide open. He stepped inside and began to look around at other visitors in the Library, and he noticed that he didn't *hear* any of them; despite the fact that they were clearly talking to their respective computers. The glass walls and doors were apparently sound-proofed. *"No need to worry about noise in THIS library"*, Miles realized with a smile.

"Welcome to General Knowledge Station #4251, how may

I help you today?" a voice, similar to the one on the main floor, greeted Miles.

"I'd like to know where I am, and learn more about the surrounding area." Miles really wasn't sure where to begin, so he figured he would start with something simple.

The terminal hummed softly and produced the information on-screen:

Location:	Main Library (4th Floor)
	280 First Street
	Amgine City
	Ontario, Canada
Date:	November 23, 2018
Government:	CAN-DO Triumvirate

"Wait…wait…" Miles uttered, causing the information on the screen to pause. This was useful information, and it revealed that he has clearly also travelled in time, a fact which did not escape his attention, but these details were not quite what he was looking for. "Please cancel my enquiry," he finished. The panel cleared and dimmed. He turned and exited the kiosk, wandering around a bit as he made his way towards the Current Events department, following the numbers to find an open terminal.

CHAPTER 8

GLOBAL UNITY MOVEMENT

After entering the first vacant booth he encountered, Miles was once again greeted warmly by the same voice, clearly one that was designed for the whole building. With a determined look in his eyes, he made his request. "I'd like to see a brief review of the major news stories and events from the past 5 years."

The screen began displaying a great deal of information: low crime rates, negligible air pollution, practically non-existent unemployment rates, consistent voter turn-outs for government elections, and no weather disasters that escaped detection or forewarning. Miles was astounded! But nothing could have prepared him for what he would see next...a sight so shocking that he requested the computer to stop displaying further data. A report on the professional wrestling scene in this world churned up an image of an athletic blonde proudly wearing a gold and black leather belt around her waist.

"A-A-Amber?!?!" he fumbled over the name on his tongue as the shock overwhelmed him, until he read the name underneath. "'The Canadian Wrestling Goddess' Faith a.k.a. Krystal Knight..." he read aloud, his eyes darting back and forth between the name and the image. "Hmmm..." he pondered openly, reading over the article detailing her accomplishments, and then reading about upcoming appearances. With some difficulty, Miles realized that he had to accept the fact that, while this woman bore an incredible resemblance to his ex-girlfriend, she could not possibly be the same person. Being a wrestling fan from a young age, he was intrigued to think what a professional wrestling event would be like in this realm, but decided to refocus his attention on finding out more from the vast resources of the Library computers.

Asking the computer to resume its previous search, Miles pored over the data being presented. There was something missing though, something he wasn't seeing in the information being provided. He saw hockey results, World Cup soccer results, even Cricket standings! Then he realized something was amiss, and uttered his next question,

"Which country won the Olympics this year?"

The screen went dark as the computer seemed to take a bit longer to process this query. The screen lit up again, but it was blank! The Library Computer voice said, "There is no match for your enquiry in Library records."

Miles was confused again, as he pursed his lips thoughtfully and wondered *"What happened to the Olympics?"* Leaving the kiosk, he returned to the terminal that he had gone to originally, in the General Knowledge Department. Frustrated by his lack of understanding, he cut the computer voice's greeting short.

"What happened to the 2018 Olympic Games?"

The computer groaned and whirred, and the voice replied with the closest available response to the query provided, "The Olympic Games was a global event that started in 1896, in Athens,

Greece; and was ended after the 1994 Games, in Lillehammer, Norway."

Miles thought for a moment as he recalled the '94 Games, particularly the increased media hype and the Kerrigan/Harding scandal. *"But, there WERE more events, scandalous and otherwise, in the years that followed,"* he reminded himself.

"Why was the event halted after the 1994 Games?" Miles asked.

"A growing conglomerate of committees and groups from around the world had observed and agreed that the Olympic Games were no longer serving the event's original intent." The computer seemed to more easily respond to this question. "Concerns over political upheavals, international conflicts, further targeted assaults similar to the incident involving figure skaters Nancy Kerrigan and Tonya Harding in 1994, and a continued global financial decline led to the termination of further Olympic events."

The computer paused its report, and presented Miles with a "More" button, giving him the choice as to whether he wanted to hear a further explanation of what happened after 1994. Intrigued by what he'd learned so far, he pressed his fingers against the flashing "More" button on the touch screen, and the computer voice continued.

"During this time, it was observed that the World Cup soccer event had managed to produce a greater amount of consistent and positive global interest, as well as financial gains across the globe; and that the sport of hockey was seen benefiting from similar interest. Starting in the winter of 1996, the **Global Unity Movement** was developed.

The **Global Unity Movement (GUM)** began with the introduction of a similar "World Cup" hockey event. In keeping with the originally proposed and developed alternating structure of the Olympics in 1994, the World Cup Hockey and World Cup Soccer events were set to alternate every 2 years."

Miles couldn't believe his ears. Could this one factor be a part of how society here had developed so differently from the Earth that he knew? Upon recalling the differences that he had observed so far, compared to the Earth that he was more familiar with, he knew what his next question should be.

"It would seem that this *GUM Movement* helped the people of Earth avoid a sticky situation." He quipped, despite knowing full well that the computer terminal would be unlikely to respond to his pun. Re-embracing the seriousness of his research, he issued his next query. "What can you tell me about this 100 year age restriction?" Miles was a bit less panicked when asking this question. He felt he had a firmer grasp of how this world differed and why.

"Inquiries regarding laws related to human sciences and similar fields, including the Century Life Mandate, would be better addressed on the 9th Floor, Human Sciences Department." The computer replied.

Miles had that uneasy feeling that something was amiss again. "What section?"

"The 9th Floor is completely devoted to the study of Human Sciences." The voice informatively responded. "Any terminal on that floor will allow you to access the information that you have requested."

"A whole floor like this one, devoted solely to human science?" Miles bit his tongue so as not to ask the question aloud, instead thanking the computer again, and turning to leave.

Whilst approaching the elevators once again, he accidentally bumped into a tall, dark haired Latina woman, who was nearly knocked off her feet by the impact. Instinctively, Miles reached out for her arm to help steady her, and allow her to recover her balance.

"Oh, I am SO sorry! I was not expecting…well, that is to say that…" the svelte, tanned skin beauty appeared very flustered by the incident. "Never mind, I just…I was not paying attention to where I was going," she tried again before letting out a calming sigh, "I apologize."

Miles smiled politely, "I'm just glad that neither of us got hurt from the impact and that I was able to help keep you from falling onto the floor."

The befuddled lady blushed. "Yes, thank you very much. Have a lovely afternoon." She gently pulled her arm from his grip, and proceeded on her way towards the kiosks.

Miles watched her leave, a half frown appearing on his lips as watching her walk away from him so abruptly only served to remind him of what his ex-girlfriend had done. His eyes lowered as he took a deep breath followed by a heavy sigh.

Returning his attention to his original intentions, he approached the elevators once again and entered the same car that he was in the first time. He requested to be taken to the 9th floor.

It was time for him to get the answers that Professor Archaios seemed reluctant to provide him with.

CHAPTER 9

THE NINTH FLOOR

QUANTUS ENTERPRISES:
LOBOS CHAMBER #314
12:57pm, Friday, November 23rd, 2018

The shrouded, cybernetically-enhanced figure, who had maintained a watchful eye on the monitors displaying the visuals captured by the security drone, was growing impatient. Grumbling with frustration, he turned his attention to another screen adjacent to the first. His disgruntlement was not eased by what he saw, as the second display failed to provide any additional input on the unknown visitor to Amgine City. However, it was also clear that the system was sluggish and not functioning properly.

"Damn bugs!" he muttered, finally venting his frustration by hammering his metallic fist down against a panel on the desk, managing to punch a hole through it.

Gazing more closely at the surveillance recording of Miles' journey along First Street, the mysterious man halted the playback, and closely observed the portable tablet/map in Miles' hand.

"We need to set up a remote tracker for that device." The man spoke with a more hopeful, well-educated confidence, "I want to know the MINUTE he becomes more readily available for us to apprehend him. Be careful, and be discreet, we don't want the Bullet Squad alerted to his presence, nor his potential capture."

"I will take care of it at once, Grylos" replied the female voice of a figure that had remained in the shadows, acknowledging the command with a nod. Extending a folding walking stick, the visually impaired woman gradually made her way towards the door, and disappeared from the room.

🕐🕑🕒

AMGINE CITY
MAIN LIBRARY
1:03pm Friday, November 23rd, 2018

The elevator car stopped at the 9th floor. Stepping out, Miles observed a very different feeling in the air, and a much more white and sterile appearance to the lights and walls. Outside the window directly in front of him loomed dark clouds. He moved closer to the window. It had started to rain, exactly as forecast! Looking at his tablet for the time, his eyes widened as he gasped *"Precisely on schedule!"* he thought to himself.

"Amazing!" he exclaimed aloud, unable to contain his astonishment.

Looking around sheepishly, he was suddenly very grateful for the sound-proof booths that occupied much of the floor. As he refocused on his surroundings, his eyes widened over the sheer number of information terminals, in kiosks similar to what he'd found on the 4th floor.

Determined to find answers, he strode to the nearest terminal and enquired about the "Century Life Mandate" age restriction and the developments in medical sciences that allowed mankind to regularly reach such a milestone. The information that he received shocked him.

"To think that a few simple differences in the approaches that were made during the 1990s could have led to such a vastly different world…" he reflected quietly upon what he was reading. Learning a great deal about how this realm differed from the one that he had already struggled to come to terms with!

"Human Sciences indeed!" he exclaimed openly, comforted with the knowledge that his voice wouldn't carry beyond the booth. The library computer terminal had revealed to him how such a grand percentage of the world's population had managed to reach the age of 100 and beyond; thus causing the implementation of the "Century Life Mandate". A company called Quantus Enterprises had utilized the development of human cloning technology to enhance medical science, in order to experiment and discover cures for major diseases, and their leading causes and symptoms. This Earth, or wherever he was, had worked beyond the ethical (and often abundantly religious) arguments that were laid against the use of clones in this utilitarian manner. His mind raced as he tried to imagine just how many thousands of lives might have been saved, based on the number of disease/plague/epidemic-related deaths in his home realm that he had read about over the better part of 20 years, by this one surreal scientific accomplishment.

The cumulative impact of this realization caused him to feel a bit light-headed, and he leaned somewhat heavily against the glass wall of the kiosk for a moment. As much as he wanted to learn more about the world around him, he knew he'd need to get some air, and take a walk after such a startling revelation. Finding a button that allowed him to transfer the data that resulted from his enquiry to his tablet, he proceeded to do so.

During the swift download procedure, the lights around him, and the terminal monitors, flickered and powered down. A message appeared on the screen, when emergency lighting was provided, that read:

"There is a bug in our system. We are attempting to clear it quickly and efficiently. We apologize for any inconvenience this may cause."

Miles looked down at his tablet. The download was mostly completed, but the rest would have to wait. While checking on what had successfully downloaded, Miles noticed a flashing icon and pressed it with his finger. A new window opened on the screen to reveal a live map of the immediate area outside, and the movement of the storm above. The rain was scheduled to cease in 18 minutes.

Having come to the conclusion that here was still so much more to explore than just the Library, and little more that the systems here could provide him while they were malfunctioning; he left the kiosk, and set off towards the elevators once more.

QUANTUS ENTERPRISES:
HIGH DENSITY STORAGE ROOM
1:14pm, Friday, November 23rd, 2018

Back at Quantus Enterprises, having left Anita to observe any updates on the computer tracking system, Anthony Thascalos laboured to recover some old paper files from data storage. He'd sworn that he had previously encountered or read about a phenomenon similar to what the radar trackers had detected earlier in the day; it was all too familiar to have been a fluke or coincidence. One thing was for certain, something had happened that shouldn't have, and he was going to need more information before he could provide a proper explanation and a potential solution.

CHAPTER 10

PLUMBING THE DEPTHS

AMGINE CITY:
DOWNTOWN
1:22pm, Friday, November 23rd, 2018

While the storm began to abate outside, Miles moved through the lobby until he found an empty chair and sat down to take a closer look at his tablet. Opening the map function, he tried to learn more about other places in Amgine City.

He quickly determined that he was in the middle of a vast metropolis, laid out and designed very efficiently. There were 2 sports arenas, a large air travel hub, and 3 commuter train stations; not to mention an elaborate sub-rail system. But what specifically caught Miles' eye was a bordered off area on the map, which was a great deal more faded than the vibrant colours that washed over the rest of the screen. Miles contemplated what its ominous appearance might represent, but also felt apprehension about what might result from exploring that particular region.

Miles tapped the section of the map that showed the underground sub-rail transit system. It was intricate and vast, spanning the city and beyond. *"This is what a subway system*

61

SHOULD be like!" he thought; deciding that he would visit the nearest station next, and explore more of the city that way.

The rain outside had stopped, and the clouds had begun to clear, precisely as timed in the forecast. Miles headed towards the exit. He paused, noticing how swiftly the ground panels seemed to dry up, and looked up at the sky again. Once more a flickering line of colour streaked across the sky, this time a bit more green than purple. Miles considered going back into the Library to learn what this effect was, and its purpose, but his curiosity and desire to explore were stronger than his interest in further research, and he had to remind himself that the library's systems were probably still down.

Checking the time, Miles realized that he might encounter rush hour crowds at the sub rail station. He wondered how much better or worse a rush hour crowd would be in a city where people could live to be 100 or more? Following the direction indicators on the map towards the nearest sub-rail system access point, Miles still did not realize that he was being monitored by the hovering robotic drone. He located the entrance to the station and descended the stairs towards it while the drone slowly drifted away.

Inside the station terminal, the first thing Miles noticed was not the "Fares and Information Kiosk" nor the well-marked pathways, but simply how clean the floors, walls, and even the air seemed to be down there. It was reasonably quiet for this time of day too! Upon approaching the Fares and Information Kiosk, Miles realized that he had no money! He looked around in a mild panic, but then saw a screen light up in front of him:

Welcome to the First Street Sub-Rail Station, Citizen!
To pay or redeem a fare,
Please press your thumb on the pad below:

One-Way Trip: 3 Credits, 5 Units
Day Pass: 10 Credits
Weekly Pass: 35 Credits
Monthly Pass: Not Available at this Terminal

Hesitantly, Miles pressed his right thumb to the "One-Way Trip" icon on the pad. After a few brief seconds, the gate opened in front of him, granting him access to the platform. Miles reluctantly moved towards the opening and, before he could try to determine how his thumb print could carry currency or earn him--an outsider--access, he was distracted by a humming noise. The hum gradually increased in intensity, as if something were approaching. To his relief, it was only the arrival of the sub-rail train. He watched as the doors slid open, allowing a large group of people to exit the train, before he stepped aboard.

Overwhelmed with curiosity, Miles decided to stand so he could see more of his immediate surroundings. The train ran so smoothly and quietly that he didn't realize, until three minutes after departure, that it was moving. Gazing to his left, towards the front end of the train; he was able to quickly determine that he was clearly in the lead car. He couldn't help but smile when he noticed that other passengers were using their mobile phones. The developers of the sub-rail system here had worked out a way of allowing cell phones to be used underground!

The train boasted other surprising features as well. Looking behind him, he was amazed to see that the interior of the train, rather than being separated, seemed almost endless! He couldn't see any division between the cars and the train's length was one and a half to two times longer than any he remembered at home. He surmised that this might have been called an "open concept" train, and it allowed passengers to walk freely from one end to the other.

Looking more closely at the barrier-free access between the sub-rail cars, he was also able to notice a group of small children that was running around rough-housing and climbing all over the seats in the next car. Observing them carefully, he realized that although they appeared to be laughing and speaking to each other, he heard nothing from where he was standing. Walking easily rather than lurching as he might have done on the trains where he was from, Miles moved towards the space that connected the 2 cars, and suddenly was awash in the noise of their play. There was an invisible, sound-proofed, barrier between the cars!

Onlookers watched as the only person standing in the half-empty lead car moved towards the next car and grasped his head. With a sense of mild panic, they watched as he stumbled back towards the lead car into the waiting arms of a tanned, long-legged female.

What the other passengers did not observe was the woman's quick injection of a tranquilizer into Miles' neck as she held him and stopped him from falling to the floor.

By the time the train had arrived at the next station, Miles Militis was not on board!

CHAPTER 11

MALUM CITY

CENTRUS LABORATORIES:
RESEARCH LAB #2
4:15pm, Saturday October 25th, 2014

Doctor Roger Thascalos gazed at the updated information on the screen in front of him and shook his head in disappointment.

"So now we know that something has occurred that was, apparently, highly localized, and may or may not have transported someone to somewhere...somehow." The bearded elder paused, struggling to make sense of the data that he had received. "However, not only do we not know how they travelled to wherever they ended up, but we now can't even find out where they've disappeared to!" He exclaimed, hammering his fist on the mouse pad and nearly knocking the mouse to the floor.

Meanwhile, Professor Eric Nidell was reading through some research on nocturnal phenomena and how they might relate to the powerful wind storm, determined to rationalize the data that they had received. Having compared his research with the conclusions that Dr. Thascalos had come to, he felt comfortable enough to add his perspective.

"There's an explanation for this, and the details lie within a correlation of facts from otherwise very disparate sources. We clearly need to work under the assumption that perhaps there was something significant about this particular storm that preyed upon the region where he disappeared? Maybe that person, who we now know was transported somewhere else, was experimenting with something themselves? Finding out *how* they disappeared might help us discover where they ended up."

The scientists exchanged glances once again, but before Dr. Thascalos could respond to his assistant's hypothesis, the phone rang.

"Roger Thascalos," the lead scientist answered the call, his eyes growing ever more restless as the voice on the other end of the line explained the reason for the call. "I see," Dr. Thascalos said. "Yes, we are certainly doing everything we can to look into the situation. Right, thank you!" The bearded Englishman hesitated, fighting the temptation to slam the receiver down onto the desk.

"It would seem," Dr. Thascalos started, "that there is a bug in the system; and we may not be receiving entirely accurate information as a result."

The young apprentice gave his elder associate a look of bewilderment. "That...just does not seem possible."

Dr. Thascalos directed his exasperated gaze at the doubting technician, opting to keep his thoughts to himself; his main thought being "*Sure, NOW you run out of answers!*"

A figure shrouded in the darkness of a cold, untidy room

watched as the motionless body of Miles Militis was laid down carefully in the middle of the room, and secured by his wrists and ankles. He watched as the Latina woman who carried Miles into the room gestured respectfully and promptly exited.

Her unintentional slamming of the door interrupted the eerie silence of Miles' slumber, as the figure watched his new captive jolt up on the lumpy mattress beneath him.

Miles quickly discovered, during the sudden movement, that his wrists and ankles were restricted by what felt like metal cuffs. Looking closer at the cuffs, he determined that they were shackled to the floor.

Taking in his surroundings, he knew he wasn't where he was a few minutes ago...or was it a few hours ago? He tried again to resettle himself on the uncomfortable mattress. *"Wait...mattress, not a floating cot,"* he thought, *"and chains and cuffs. One would expect this realm to have something more advanced by now."* Taking a slow deep breath, he refocused his thoughts on his new environment,. *"On the bright side,"* he concluded with some relief, *"it doesn't LOOK like a sanatorium."* A quick comparison between where he was just a few hours ago and where he found himself now were literally as different as night and day. The air was musty, the lighting was minimal, and he could hear the sound of rats skittering along the walls. Wherever he was, it was not nearly as clean as every other place that he'd been to since originally falling asleep during that violent wind storm; and even that felt like it had happened weeks ago. Reflecting back upon that night, he once again wondered what Angelique must be thinking or doing since his disappearance.

☺☺☺

THE EREBUS RESIDENCE
5:54pm, Saturday, October 25ᵗʰ, 2014

Jack Erebus returned home earlier than expected, having finished his film work ahead of schedule. He rushed to return and surprise Angelique, but instead it was he who was surprised. He approached the house after having noticed that a great deal of the planned repair work on the outer wall remained unfinished. Looking over the damaged areas, and then seeing all of the leaves on the ground, he assumed that there was a weather-related reason that the work remained incomplete. As he passed one particular section of the outer wall, he failed to notice a faint glow emanating from an opening within it.

Jack fumbled for his keys, unlocked the door, and entered to find Angelique kneeling on the floor and staring blankly into space. Dropping his suitcase to the floor, his concern was evident as he rushed to her side.

"Angie? Angel? Sweetie, are you alright?" he gently shook her by the shoulder, but she did not acknowledge him. She remained almost trance-like, her face very pale. He felt her forehead for potential fever, and checked her pulse, noticing the floor was littered with discarded tissues. Whatever had occurred in his absence, he would not find out about it from Angie until she recovered. Cradling her in his arms, he carefully reached for his cell phone, and called for an ambulance.

☺☺☺

CENTRUS LABORATORIES:
EXPERIMENTAL SCIENCES DEPARTMENT
6:06pm, Saturday, October 25th, 2014

The return of Jack Erebus from Greece did not escape the attention of the cloaked figure named Lupo, After all, he had been maintaining surveillance on the Erebus household, where an unknown, almost mystical event had clearly taken place. A part of him still hoped that the mysterious occurrence was not related to the experiment that he had given the "go ahead" for. The man's eyes narrowed at the video screen, as he pointed an aged finger at the image of Jack.

"What the hell is *he* doing there?" Lupo growled to himself. He wasted little time punching a few commands and queries into his computer's keyboard, determined to find answers. The realization and resolution of the issues that he had encountered during the test phase of his experiment would have to wait.

☺☺☺

2:08pm, Friday, November 23rd, 2018

As Miles took in the area around him, he saw a figure sitting in the shadows near the mattress where he lay. A wrinkled hand arose from the darkness, and light bloomed in a bare bulb hanging over dangling chains. It brightened the room, but didn't improve it much. The decor remained barren and simplistic. Now he could see the old figure better, his wrinkled skin brown--African-American, possibly, sitting on the edge of an old wooden rocking chair.

The man just watched him quietly; there was an odd twinkle in his eye. He broke the silence by finally addressing his new guest.

"So, you are the latest unknown variable, the mystery man that our surveillance trackers picked up." The old man started, "we could find no information on you in any of our records." His eyes wandered appraisingly over Miles' outfit. "Though, it seems like you have managed to fit right in with the rest of the Utopians...*almost!*"

"Utopians?" Miles interrupted. "Wha...huh?"

"It is how we here refer to those who live outside our district." The older man said with a smile. "The ones who take in all the garbage that the reigning government feeds them, without question."

"One man's garbage is another man's gospel." Miles replied, attempting to sound intelligently philosophical and understanding.

The old man's eyes widened, a grin crossing his lips. He noted the calm demeanour of his bound captive, despite the tense uncertainty of this new situation. He gestured to someone else in the room, and pointed towards the bindings that held Miles' wrists and ankles. Miles recognized the same Latina woman whom he'd bumped into at the Library; a discovery that almost made him smile, until he realized that she clearly must have walked into him intentionally! *Was "surveillance tracker" another word for "spy"?"* he wondered.

"Let's get you out of those bindings." The old man broke the silence, and Miles' fixation on his sultry assistant. "You aren't exactly a prisoner here; we just couldn't be certain about how you would react to us, and needed to take precautions."

Miles nodded to acknowledge his understanding, and to silently express appreciation, as his wrists and ankles were freed.

Sitting up on the edge of the mattress, he slowly swung his legs down over the edge and stretched a bit, before introducing himself.

"My name is Miles, Miles Militis," he said. "I honestly don't know how I came to be in Amgine City; but it seemed to be in my best interests for me to at least APPEAR as if I belonged there... er...here." He couldn't help but appear uncertain and confused about where he was.

"That makes sense." The older man just smiled and nodded back. "No point in trying to answer questions, when you are still trying to figure things out for yourself, especially when they tend to be regarding the same subjects!"

The quiet and long-legged subordinate returned from another room with a tray of fresh vegetables and water, resting it on the table next to Miles. He discovered that she was not only athletically built, but clearly light on her feet; he didn't even realize that she'd left the room after freeing him of his restraints. The elderly man politely waved her off, and then returned his attention to their mysterious guest.

"By the way, my name is Josef Aros." He started plainly then gestured to his companion. "This lovely young lady, who rather abruptly made your acquaintance in her efforts to help bring you to us, is Velvet."

Velvet stepped forward and bowed her head in a polite greeting toward Miles; who returned the favour, with a smile. He observed what he thought might have been a playful wink from the silent assistant. His ponderings on this potential were interrupted by his host's continued dialogue.

"As for your uncertainty with the geography of this area," Josef continued. "It really depends upon who you ask. In the original design of the land divisions and districts, this area WAS meant to be a part of Amgine City. However, the way we live our lives here is very different from the Utopians. So we were subsequently culled together, and outcast to this one specific part of the land. You are now in Depravus Tower, located in the heart of Malum City."

Miles was in the midst of taking in the cool, refreshing spring water, nearly choking on some of it when he heard the name "Malum City". Miles was a reasonably well educated man; he knew almost instantly that "Malum" was Latin for "Evil". As he reached that conclusion, his eyes met those of his host, and saw the gleam in Mr. Aros' eye, the elder's eyebrows furling.

"Don't let the name concern you," Josef tried to reassure his seemingly anxious guest, "it wasn't one we chose for ourselves. We are not predominantly malevolent, Mr. Militis; we are merely different. There are some ideals by which we cannot abide, and so we are outcast as rebels, and looked upon as borderline criminals. To many, we are disaffectionately referred to as The Bullet Squad, despite our tendency to avoid violence."

The discussion was abruptly interrupted by the sound of an old fashioned rotary telephone ringing. Josef paused and looked around, reaching to his left for the vintage style phone.

"Hello?" Josef answered. Miles was astonished to find such an old fashioned communications device in use. Between the old style phones, the rough mattresses, and the bare hanging bulbs, he speculated whether these Malum City dwellers were perhaps so rebellious that they were…anti-technology?

He could not understand the voice on the other end of the line, but it sounded like a younger man speaking, and doing so in an urgent manner.

As he listened, Josef Aros's expression quickly shifted from pleasant calmness to almost a look of despair and his eyes lost their twinkle. The older man's hand almost lost its grip on the phone, but he managed to recover it as he stared blankly in Miles' direction to continue his phone conversation. .

"Assemble a team, two groups of 3 or 4, and find out exactly where the MOTH Squad are headed." Josef instructed the panicked-sounding young man on the other end of the line, "And double check the facts; we don't want to mess it up like what happened last time. Those people aren't doing anything so terrible that they deserve the fate that the Utopians' government would enforce upon them."

Josef hung up the phone, his expression having become rather grim.

"We have a problem, and our discussion is going to have to be put on the back burner." Joseph quipped sternly. "The MOTH Squad Enforcement Team has found some new targets, and we have a less than 20 minute window in which to save them!"

CHAPTER 12

THE MOTH SQUAD

"MOTH Squad?" Miles repeated curiously.

Josef frowned, returning his attention to his guest.

"It's one of the most troubling aspects of the CAN-DO Triumvirate's Utopian Society." Josef's voice was noticeably a tad bitter as he elaborated on this subject. "I'm not sure if you are familiar with a movement, originally designed to trigger a global awakening and awareness with regards to energy conservation and environmental preservation, known as Earth Hour?"

Miles was even more confused. "Yes, I'm familiar with Earth Hour. It happens in the early spring, usually sometime in late March."

"It will indeed be very interesting to learn where you come from, and how you came to be here now." Josef said, seeming fascinated by the reaction. "However, I suppose I should just tell you how things differ here. The Earth Hour event is a bi-monthly worldwide occurrence. It is initiated towards the end of the odd numbered months, six times a year. Its basis and purpose are benevolent, but its enforcement has become very strict and unyielding."

"This MOTH Squad is...an Earth Hour Enforcement Squad?" Miles interrupted.

With a sigh, Josef nodded again.

"That's basically what they are, yes. In fact, that might be precisely what they are referred to as by the Utopians. We prefer to call them the MOTH Squad, which stands for "My way Or The Highway", because of the arbitrary approach that they use to enforce the once basic, and well-meaning principles behind the event." Josef paused and then sighed again.

"I suppose it's not as bad as it could be, but it really shouldn't be handled in this manner at all. In my 120 plus years on the planet, I've never encountered such an extreme misuse of technological advancements; particularly those that have been discovered or created over the past 25 years."

Miles eyed his companion carefully. "Wait! *You* are over 120 years old?"

Josef nodded, "Yes, but, one thing at a time...we need to handle this emergency first. The MOTH Squad will find and approach their target in less than 15 minutes." He rose from his chair, and gestured towards Miles. "Follow me, perhaps you can be of help to us."

Miles was having trouble keeping up with the information overload, and the subtle but profound differences between his world and this one. He did his best to follow Josef.

As the older man led him through numerous hallways and rooms, and entire sections that were labelled and painted in distinctively different ways, Miles realized that Depravus Tower was clearly much larger than he had initially anticipated it being.

Finally, Josef led Miles into a room littered with flickering consoles and colourful electronic panels, some that looked like they were 20 years old, although others appeared to be more modern technological devices. The room was organized in such a way that it resembled a museum of technology, except these exhibits were fully functional. *"Clearly not anti-technology then,"* Miles told himself.

As Miles tried to adjust to his new surroundings and see what he might understand or recognize from the array of large video monitors that occupied the longest wall in the room, Josef greeted a slender man seated in front of them. He looked to be in his early 20's.

"What's the story, Tim?" Josef asked.

"We've confirmed that there are people living in 2 houses, on a side street about 10 blocks away, openly planning on not partaking in the Earth Hour movement." Tim said in a crisp Welsh accent, "Our contact inside the Quantus building verifies that they are about ready to make a move to apprehend the inhabitants of those 2 residences."

"So there's an Earth Hour event tonight?" Miles asked, but almost wished that he hadn't when he noticed the looks that both Tim and Josef were giving him.

"No, this is for Sunday evening." Tim responded in a firm tone. "The MOTH Squad has been using a good portion of its technological budget to foresee any threats, diversions, or attempted alterations to the global plans and initiatives of the CAN-DO Triumvirate, and the world government as a whole. They've been using some very sophisticated means of surveillance to that end. Unfortunately, we don't have their funds or their resources, and they often attempt to randomize the timing of their insurgent efforts; which only makes our job more difficult." Tim felt at liberty to elaborate further on what was happening and why, having trusted Josef's decision to bring a stranger into the control room.

"Which is why," Josef added, "I wanted Tim to make doubly sure of the facts this time. Our last insurgent effort to rescue some innocents ended in disaster because we received inaccurate data, and went out in force to the wrong location, at the wrong time. It was embarrassing, costly, and frustrating."

"Not to mention," Tim uttered abruptly, "a threat to our security, and the security of Malum City as a whole!"

Miles sat down hard in a nearby chair, trying to process the information that he had been given during the past 30 minutes. He suddenly wondered if the odd streaks of colour he had observed in the sky had anything to do with the MOTH Squad's technologies that allowed them insight into "crimes" that were not yet being committed.

Josef glanced at Miles, observing how overwhelmed that he seemed to be, and frowned slightly. Returning his attention to the monitor, he addressed Tim once again.

"Alright, get your people ready." Josef started issuing directions for the rescue operation. "I want you to instruct the 2 Retrieval Vehicles to be in that area. I was going to send Miles here as additional back-up, but I think that he's got too much on his mind already, and there's still a great deal that I need to discuss with him."

Miles was naturally curious about how they would go about non-violently preventing the altercation, but accepted Josef's analysis of the situation, and understood that he would get some needed and welcomed answers in the forthcoming discussion. In the meantime, he stood to observe the preparations being made, and the analytical data appearing on the screen regarding the details of how the Enforcement Squad even knew about the intentions of citizens so far in advance! *"Could THIS be how Amgine City has kept itself so clean?"* Miles pondered quietly. *"Being able to observe future threats, and other events, and determine actions to avoid/prevent them BEFORE they occur?"*

Just as Miles was preparing to leave the room, Tim called Josef over a 2-way radio. The young man had already made his way towards the parking garage.

"Josef, we're a man short," the radio crackled. "If there's any way you can see about sending the new fellow out with us, I think we can make sure that he doesn't get too overwhelmed."

Miles listened to Tim on the radio, and looked over at Josef, who looked up from the console and back at Miles. Receiving a nod of consent, and being directed towards the same door that Tim exited through, Miles hesitantly nodded back and followed the direction provided, which led to an underground parking garage.

Most of the cars down there didn't have visible locking mechanisms either, an observation that he was definitely still curious about. Tim waved Miles over to the car that he was in, and opened the door from the inside, allowing Miles easy access to the hovering vehicle. The safety belt immediately came forward, and secured itself firmly but not too tightly across Miles chest and waist. Even this little bit of unfamiliar technology only added to the more delightful element of surprise that Miles felt as he could help but quote Little Orphan Annie openly, "I think I'm gonna like it here!"

Tim snapped his head towards his new passenger with a quizzical look, but then pulled out of the space and sped out towards the exit of the garage.

"Look, we've got 6 minutes, and our target destination is about 10 blocks away, so please keep all of your comments and questions to a minimum until the job is done. Understood?" Tim instructed. Miles simply nodded, sat quietly, and watched as the unfamiliar streets and sights of the ever-more-wondrous city raced past his window.

After finally arriving at the designated area, Tim slowed the vehicle and parked outside a simple looking bungalow. Surveying the immediate area, he then glanced at the target address; shaking his head as he studied the residence.

"Ugh, another one of those "Trapped in the 50's" types…" Tim muttered. "More often than not, the ones I get sent out to pick up are non-conformists living in some kind of old fashioned "retro" style dwelling like this one." Disengaging the engine, Tim exited the vehicle, and directed Miles and the occupants of the 2 other vehicles to do the same.

"You two will stay by the vehicles," gesturing to each group, Tim started issuing directions. "You two will take care of the house next door, Miles and I will go towards the front door of this one."

The other team members acknowledged their orders and began to get into position.

Tim watched as the other team members acknowledged their orders and moved to get into position. He led Miles to the front door of the closer residence, and rang the doorbell. A light on the other side of the door illuminated, a few moments later. A lock could be heard being deactivated as the door opened to reveal a middle-aged Asian couple. The couple eyed the visitors with a mixture of awe and bewilderment.

"Good evening sir, ma'am," Tim greeted the residents. "We're here on behalf of your local government, on important official business. I must ask that you both come with us right away. I can assure you that it is for your own safety."

Before the couple could adequately respond to the request, Tim's radio crackled.

"Team Leader, we've got company! There's a vortex forming at the southern intersection. Team members Charlie and Delta have successfully gathered the members of the second household into their vehicle."

Tim sighed at the news of his time running ever so short; glaring at the couple who seemed more interested in trying to lean in different directions in an effort to look behind their new guests to see who else was coming, than in complying with his simple request.

"Alright listen; we don't have a lot of time for explanations or hesitation on this." Tim was losing his composure, and his patience, with this suspiciously quiet couple. "If you are willing to let us help you and protect you, we need to go *now*!"

The couple gazed at each other briefly. The man shrugged and reached back to turn off the light, an ironic gesture to say the least. They scurried past Tim and Miles, as the door automatically closing and locking behind them. Tim signalled to Miles to return to the vehicle, and then spoke into his radio:

"Alright, all teams…all teams, return to your vehicles. We've apprehended the targets, and we've got less than two minutes before we potentially become targets ourselves!"

With barely 20 seconds to spare, the three car team sped out of the neighbourhood as the previously announced spatial vortex drifted towards the target residence, and opened up on the front lawn. Helmeted figures carefully surveyed the vicinity as they approached the front door. A high tech scanner was being used on the front door, working to overpower and deactivate the lock. However, within a minute of the lock becoming disabled, the team of helmeted men and women were signalled to return towards the vortex that had all but closed behind them: their objectives were no longer present.

HUMBER MEMORIAL HOSPITAL
8:24pm, Saturday, October 25th, 2014

Jack Erebus was an overtired, and frustrated, emotional wreck as he sat in the waiting area of the local hospital. After quite some time, the physician in charge of his wife's care approached him.

"We've examined your wife, Mr. Erebus," the medic began.

"There is no evidence of physical abuse or injury. She has remained in an inexplicable, borderline vegetative state, and has not yet responded to any stimulus. There is no clear indication as to what has caused this to occur, but our best guess would have to be some form of emotional or psychological trauma"

Jack tried to feel a bit better about the situation, the fact that the cause of his loving wife's unresponsive condition was not likely to be due to physical abuse or an accident. But there were still too many uncertainties regarding the true cause and explanation, and this only added to the stress he had dealt with since returning home.

🕐🕑🕒

CENTRUS LABORATORIES:
RESEARCH LAB #2
12:21am, Sunday, October 26th, 2014

Dr. Roger Thascalos tried to maintain his composure, but was struggling to fully comprehend the information that his younger assistant was trying to impart to him. He had heard some unique terms and scientific gobbledygook in his time, but this latest data had blown his mind.

"So, what you are trying to tell me is that the wind storm on Saturday morning, was not supposed to be THAT severe, and that it was influenced by some force beyond Nature; creating some kind of temporal or trans-dimensional transference?"

"That's what the data has been telling me, based on my comparative researches with previous phenomena of this kind." Eric replied with a slow nod. "I have a hunch that it might have something to do with an attempted manipulation of the gravitational waves that Albert Einstein theorized about. However,

I will have to look further into the details of that theory, and any more recent findings on the subject, to figure out if they could play a factor in this situation. Mind you, manipulation on such a grand scale is almost impossible to imagine."

"Can you elaborate on this further?" Dr. Thascalos queried, trying to get a better handle on what Eric was trying to tell him. "What about these gravitational waves?"

"From what I can recall, from my initial studies on the subject, Einstein theorized that space-time was actually a 4th dimension combining the two elements that were once believed to be separate. He contradicted Newton's theory of how gravity worked, and determined that each object in the universe had its own gravitational pull. By their movements, and by their very existence, objects would alter the placement and trajectory of space-time around them, causing ripples...or waves. While these waves are generally considered to be rather weak and highly localized, the manipulation of large, and more particularly, celestial objects to the right extent could have quite incredible ramifications on other objects in their path and/or vicinity. However, as I stated earlier, the chances of someone managing to combine the force of waves from a group of objects that massive to develop such a phenomenon are highly unlikely."

As unbelievable as this potential epiphany was, it *did* bring them one step closer to determining the details behind the disappearance of the unknown male; and perhaps, where he might have disappeared to.

CHAPTER 13

TOUCHING BASE

It was another quiet ride back, as Miles was returned to Depravus Tower, where he first met Josef, and got out of the car near the front door, where he saw his elderly host waiting for him. Moments later, he watched as Tim's car and the other two vehicles sped away. Taking a moment to observe his surroundings, Miles was almost hesitant, after all that he had experienced in such a short time span, about making his way towards Josef, and the door.

"Some mighty impressive technology in those vehicles; similar to the ones I saw on First Street." Miles said in greeting.

"Yes, I'm assuming that you will have some questions about that as well." Josef smiled, seemingly relaxed again; particularly after hearing about the success of the mission. "Come on in, and by the way, congratulations on your first successful rescue operation." Josef leaned back to hold the door open for Miles, who was rather surprised that it wasn't automated, like so many other doors seemed to be.

Miles stepped towards the open door, when he caught sight of another cascading ripple of a white, almost crystalline colour shimmering across the night sky. He paused, and tried to follow the bright band of sparkling white, turning away from Josef for a moment.

"Did you see that?" He asked. "What *is* that?" The unusual cascading ripple faded long before his elderly host had the chance to look up and catch sight of anything but the sky's plain, rather dark, appearance.

"I saw nothing." Josef replied with a half frown. He shook his head and sighed, "C'mon inside, it was probably just a reflection of something."

Miles frowned. He seemed to be the only person to have noticed the effect all three times. He turned back towards his host and entered the open door.

"Thank you, Josef; the rescue effort was quite an experience." Miles opted to start afresh as he pulled a chair near Josef's rocking chair, and sat down. "What would've happened to those people if the MOTH Squad had caught up with them first?"

Josef sat back in the rocking chair and sighed. The idea of another rescue effort failing, clearly, did not sit well with him.

"They would've been arrested, penalized, possibly jailed." Josef replied.

"They'd arrest people for not turning out their lights during Earth Hour?" Miles asked incredulously.

"That's the tricky thing about developing a Utopian society; the incongruences are dealt with much more harshly, particularly for those who attempt to subvert *"Paradise."* A perfect world is a dream many are bound to share, but it all too often ends up being led by someone, or a group of individuals, who cannot handle the seemingly unforeseen elements that don't abide by the example provided by the majority. Non-compliance simply is not tolerated, no matter how ideal a society may attempt to become." Josef paused, "Now, on to other matters. I believe that you had some questions regarding the hover cars?"

"Yes," Miles nodded, realizing that a change of subject was clearly in order. "It might seem naive of me, but I didn't see any door locking mechanisms. I accept that this society has worked very hard towards perfecting itself, and prolonging its existence and the lifespan of its individual inhabitants. But, there are clearly bound to be some people, even in this utopian society, that rebel against the established laws and codes..." Miles paused, realizing that he would have to choose his next words carefully; so as not to offend his host. Clearing his throat, he resumed, "Excuse me, about the laws and codes which I am more familiar with? Don't people try to break in and steal other people's cars here?"

"Oh, the doors are seldom locked anymore." Josef replied, stifling a chuckle. "The gas caps on the hover cars have a built in combination lock and fingerprint reader. Any attempt to steal a hover car would only last as long as the fuel remaining in the tank, because nobody would be able to fill up a gas tank that wasn't their own, or didn't have their fingerprint scan on an authorization list."

"That's ingenious!" Miles exclaimed with an admiring nod.

"Alright," Miles hesitated a bit, took a deep breath, and then continued. "I was told a little about the Century Life Mandate, and that there were special conditions for those looking to live beyond the age of 100. You have admitted to me that you are over 120 years of age. The gentleman who informed me of the Century Life Mandate, but not the basis behind it, indicated that there were those who attempted to subvert the law, and work around the conditions. I'm assuming that's why you are here?" Miles tried not to wince, but he really wished he'd phrased it more gently. He was already beating himself over it, even before receiving the response.

"The Century Life Mandate is a crock." Josef uttered with similar frivolity of expression, eyeing his new, curious friend carefully. "It's just another part of the Triumvirate's efforts to maintain some kind of control over society as a whole. Yes, there are those of us who have reached and/or surpassed the age of 100, and have refused to terminate our lives simply because we have not established ourselves as having made a "significant impact" on society or the world. If choosing to live life, until Nature or Fate determines that our time is up, is a crime; then I'd rather be guilty but *free*."

Miles looked befuddled, "The CAN-DO Triumvirate tries to control how the whole world operates?" His confusion somewhat tempered as he watched the older man shake his head.

"No, no, sorry, perhaps I misspoke." Josef answered while leaning back in his chair and rocking a bit His tone was much more relaxed now. "The CAN-DO Triumvirate is just a regional government chapter for the country, not the world. It *is*, however, an important part of the Whole Earth Decisive Operatives Organization (WE-DOO). Like most governing bodies on the planet, there are 3 chosen/elected leaders who determine law and the allocation of funds, services, resources, etc. Sometimes it's just easier to say "The Triumverate" to describe different government chapters."

Miles found himself having difficulty discerning whether he'd finally gotten more answers than questions, or if he'd ended up with still more questions left unanswered. Opting to stay on the same line of questions, he posed the next one based on a curious observation.

"What is the purpose behind the company logos that appear to be on many of the hover vehicles that I have observed on the streets of Amgine City?"

The older man smiled and then sighed softly. "Even in a "Utopian society", it can be difficult for some people to be able to make ends meet. Companies willingly pay drivers and car owners, a small amount per month for advertising via sporting a logo on their vehicle."

Miles sat up suddenly, having come to the logical conclusion that this stipend would probably be paid through a person's touch; which would then explain the fingerprint payment at the sub-rail station. But, before he could speak up to verify his assumption, the momentary silence was interrupted by a faint ringing sound.

Rising quickly from his seat, Miles realized that it was coming from his tablet. Watching Josef leave the room, he pressed the flashing icon on the portable computer. A familiar voice emanated almost immediately from the built-in speaker.

"Mr. Militis? It's Professor Archaios, from the Scientific Unity Complex." The voice of the Professor was crystal clear, despite how small the speaker on the tablet appeared to be. Miles didn't have time to evaluate why the Professor, who openly admitted preferring to refer to it as simply *"The Complex"* would suddenly opt to mention its full name, before the voice spoke again. "When you have time, I would appreciate you returning to the Complex to see me. We might have unearthed some new information that might help explain how you came to be here with us in Amgine City."

CHAPTER 14

PROJECT WELTSCHMERZ

Miles could think of no real reason to decline the invitation, particularly since he was eager to learn more about the means of his arrival in this strange land, and readily accepted.

"I will try to make my way back over there in the next few hours, Professor." He replied. "Thank you very much for contacting me about this." Miles pressed the icon again to end the conversation. Taking a quick look around the room, he headed towards the exit to find Josef. He nearly jumped as the elderly host stepped up to him from a shadowy corner in the hall, startling the younger man. A look of semi-suspicious concern pressed tightly, like a mask, on Mr. Aros' face.

"I can have Velvet take you back to the city," Josef offered. "But I need your assurances that you will not disclose what you have seen here. So far, you have managed to earn my trust, and I don't want to discover that that trust has been misplaced."

Miles nodded, extending his right hand to shake Josef's. "You most definitely have my solemn oath that I will not attempt to endanger what you all have worked so hard to achieve here." His handshake was readily accepted, as Josef gestured with his free hand, and Velvet stepped out into the light in response.

"Come with me, Miles," she requested, her exotic accent stifling a soft purr as she strode on ahead towards the parking lot. "I'll take you as near as I dare go to the Complex."

☉☉☉

QUANTUS ENTERPRISES:
HISTORICAL ARCHIVES
3:52pm, Friday, November 23rd, 2018

Administrator Thascalos led his new assistant Anita O'Dell to the Historical Archives section of the building. While still uncertain as to the "how" or "why", Thascalos felt that he had a better grip on the "when", and whether or not he was imagining having seen readings and information regarding a similar trans-dimensional phenomenon in the past.

"So…" he opened, after reading through some few remaining hard copy files. He raised a specially marked and monogrammed file folder that was hidden within a plain looking manila-coloured folder. The folder had a somewhat scorched appearance in some parts, as if someone had tried incinerating the file, without success. "This *has* happened before!" The Administrator proclaimed with a sense of relieved pride. Tossing aside the manila folder, he broke the seal on the previously hidden file that was clearly and colourfully labelled as "**PROJECT WELTSCHMERZ**". Thumbing through some of the more relevant documents in the folder, he nodded slowly; almost with a sense of confident understanding. "Most of the paper files that have not been scanned or otherwise converted into digital format are just personnel files and legal settlements. However, this file is neither one!

This information appears to have been deliberately misfiled. It seems clear to me that someone didn't want to acknowledge the occurrence of this phenomenon the first time." After a pause, with the Administrator stroking his chin, he concluded, "There's only one thing for it. We will have to find them!"

"Find who?" Anita asked.

The older man's beady eyes darted back towards her,

"We need to find the person who is responsible for this misfiling, and these burn marks. I have a feeling they may have more information than what has been documented on the previous transference, but was not kept in this folder." He replied. "We also need to find the man who was brought here by such unorthodox means. That is assuming, of course, that they aren't the same person." Anthony paused to consider that shocking possibility, then continued. "Either way, we now have proof that this phenomenon has happened here before. Finding this latest visitor might shed some light on facts that could not be discovered the first time. I'm going to the Glider Control Room, to see if the Quantus Enterprises air glider has captured any recent footage of our mysterious man."

Before Anita could ask her next question, the Administrator was out of the room, having darted out to find the answers that he needed.

AMGINE CITY:
DOWNTOWN
5:16pm, Friday, November 23rd, 2018

Velvet drove Miles to within a block of the Scientific Unity

Complex, just south of the Library. Miles was pleased to see some semi-familiar surroundings again, and to be back in Amgine City.

"Thank you Velvet," Miles said. "How do I go about staying in touch with you or Josef?"

"We've remotely added an entry into the Contacts list on your tablet." The hazel eyed Latin vixen replied with a playful smirk. "However, if we need to find you, we will find a way." She purred at him almost flirtatiously, and triggered the control to open the door for Miles to exit.

He smiled at her response. Reflecting back on their first "accidental" encounter, and how he'd wished he'd handled it better, he opted to attempt something that he seldom could bring himself to try, under "normal" circumstances.

"Would you like to go out for a drink sometime, or something?" He tried to control the anxiety in his voice, hoping that she would not make him wait long for a reply.

She smiled even more widely.

"I'd like that," she spoke softly, after gazing deeply into the gentleman's eyes. "Perhaps after you have met with the Professor, you can contact me?"

Miles nodded. "Okay, yes, certainly, thank you." He paused, as he turned to leave the vehicle, he looked back towards her once more "I'll see you soon."

He closed the door and, as he waited for Velvet to drive off, and was about to give a polite wave, he suddenly saw yet another cascading ripple of colour across the dark night sky. This one seemed wider than previous occurrences, and more defined; this one had a more solid, crystalline appearance.

"Hey Velvet, what is that? Did you see...?" But before he could ask her, she'd driven away. It was logical to assume that, even in the fair-minded and pacified Utopia of Amgine City, there'd still be some elements that would react negatively towards an unidentified vehicle in the centre of town, particularly at night.

Miles frowned and sighed. Whatever it was that he was seeing in the sky, it was becoming more frequent, larger, and more pronounced. He finally peeled his gaze away from the sky, and took a moment to reacquaint himself with his surroundings. Swiftly, he crossed the quiet street towards the large and rather oddly shaped Complex. Battling his inner curiosity regarding the unique exterior of the building, something he hadn't stopped to notice when he first stepped out onto the streets of Amgine City.

This time, he found Professor Archaios' office with very little difficulty.

The Professor observed his approach on a security monitor, and activated the switch to open the door to his office remotely; welcoming his guest with a warm smile.

"Welcome back, Mr. Militis! I'm not sure where you were, when I contacted you, we have discovered a bug in our tracking system software. But, I trust that you have found our fair city interesting?"

"'interesting' would be quite an understatement, Professor; 'awe-inspiring' would be more accurate." Miles responded, returning the Professor's smile. The clean air, friendly people, accurate weather forecasts, incredibly advanced Library, and a fast, quiet, and efficient sub-rail system…" his voice trailed off as he recalled the events that took place during, and shortly after, his pre-empted trip on the sub-rail train.

Archaios nodded amiably, "Very good, very good indeed. I'm glad you have enjoyed your time exploring Amgine City. I'm sorry to have interrupted it. However, I felt that you would be interested in the developments that we have made in determining the means by which you found yourself here." The Professor directed him to a chair.

The Professor looked exhausted as he gazed warily at Miles.

"We don't have ALL of the information yet, nor do we really know if there are any other answers to *be* found, but we have our most talented people working on this," The Professor said. "It would appear that your being here was not the result of some sort of malevolent or provocative behaviour. From what my colleagues and I can string together, so far, your presence here is merely the by-product of an experiment gone awry. We don't know who initiated the experiment to trigger this anomaly or if there is a way to get you back to where you belong, but we do know that your being here *has* been observed by other agencies in Amgine City, and likely beyond."

Miles sat as calmly as he could, but this news was absolutely shocking for him to hear. It was one thing for him to believe that he was transported to this realm for some specific purpose; diabolical or otherwise. But, it was a whole other thing to be confronted with the revelation of his transference being in error; or some kind of unplanned side effect. After a deep breath, he felt he should at least acknowledge that he had heard what Professor told him.

"That is alarming, but also somewhat fascinating. I suppose my next logical question would be: What should I do now?"

An extended hush followed this enquiry; both men occasionally exchanging brief glances a few times, as they each pondered a plausible response. The Professor's mouth gaped open momentarily, leaning forward, his eyes widening with a potential "Eureka!" moment, as if he were ready to reveal some kind of answer, but then he hesitated and shook his head, leaning back into his chair to ponder some more.

QUANTUS ENTERPRISES:
GLIDER CONTROL ROOM
5:33pm, Friday November 23rd, 2018

Administrator Thascalos watched as Anita entered the room. His face looked grim as he leaned back in his office chair, pondering the meaning of what he had discovered. "If what I have reviewed of the footage from the glider is completely accurate," the Administrator addressed his companion. "Our mystery man is as confused as we are with regards to how and why he is here." Adjusting the image on the screen, rolling back to a previous time sequence, he pointed to direct her attention to the visual display. "Whoever he is, it seems that the Scientific Unity Complex is his safe haven. Our glider has discovered him there at least twice so far, since his arrival was first detected."

"Scientific Unity Complex…" Anita repeated softly, almost calculatingly, her eyes fixated on the building depicted on the screen. "Hmmm, there's something strangely familiar about the shape and markings of that building." The Administrator could see the wheels spinning in her mind, her eyes fixed intently on the uniquely designed edifice. Finally shaking her head, she redirected her attention to Anthony. "What shall we do with this information?"

"The Complex itself might be worthy of investigation," The older man replied, before pushing up out of his chair, and turning towards the exit leading to the hall. "I think I should also consult with one or 2 other department heads regarding this. If you'd like to continue observing the video footage from the glider, perhaps you'll find something that I have overlooked?"

Anita nodded and then focused more carefully on the screen, rolling back the footage to the start of the previous day, when Miles first arrived.

☉☉☉

QUANTUS ENTERPRISES:
LOBOS CHAMBER #314
6:45pm, Friday, November 23rd, 2018

Grylos, the shrouded cybernetic man who had been carefully observing Miles since he left the Scientific Unity Complex, received a report, confirming that the tracker on Miles' tablet indicated his return to the Complex. While looking over details on how Miles got there, he also noticed the Quantus Glider hovering in the vicinity of the unusually shaped Complex as well.

"Suddenly everyone sees and knows TOO MUCH!" he proclaimed with an angry hiss. Rising from his Throne-like chair, he swiftly turned towards the door leading to the next room. "I want a data extraction on that mobile device immediately!" He commanded his now-silent blind companion, who nodded again, and moved to set up the extraction.

CHAPTER 15

ILLUSIONS

SCIENTIFIC UNITY COMPLEX:
PROFESSOR OLIM ARCHAIOS' OFFICE
7:02pm, Friday, November 23rd, 2018

Miles Militis and Professor Archaios remained silent for what seemed like a long 10 minutes. Neither of them could think of the right way to proceed.

Miles was not fond of extended, somewhat awkward, silences; particularly when he was the one to unintentionally initiate it. He let his mind wander, reviewing the events he'd experienced since he awoke in his current strange surroundings.

"What is the Quantus Enterprises?" he asked, breaking the prolonged silence.

"How do *you* know about the Quantus Enterprises?" The professor asked, guardedly.

Miles bit his bottom lip, wondering if he'd misspoken somehow. "When I was out travelling, I saw a blimp, or something, that had that name highlighted upon the scrolling marquee."

The Professor nodded. "Oh, I see…"

"Also," Miles added. "I noticed something else when I looked up at the sky. I had meant to find some information about it at the Library."

Professor Archaios quickly interrupted, "Oh, so you found the Library did you? That's very good. I have no doubts that you managed to find some of the answers that you were looking for there."

Miles couldn't help but notice how determined The Professor seemed to cling to the subject of the library rather than the phenomenon that he was about to describe. But he was determined to discover what it was that he had seen on several occasions since his arrival.

"Professor, on 4 separate occasions, I have noticed an unusual streak of lights, or some kind of illumination, cascading across the sky. It's like nothing I've ever seen before, and the variety of colours that I've seen so far, plus the fact that it doesn't always travel in the same direction… it doesn't seem to have a natural pattern!"

"I'm not entirely familiar with what you are describing," Professor Archaios started. "But I'm sure there's a simple explanation for it. Perhaps it is something that the OIC Group is working on?"

"I'm sorry," Miles said, sounding much more calm and controlled, despite sensing a hint of concern in the old man's voice. He felt as if Olim was almost desperate to provide a logical explanation that could satisfy his curiosity. He laboured to remain focused as he worked his mind around this new bit of information. "Who or what is the OIC Group?"

"Ah, of course, you might not have heard of them yet." The Professor was very understanding as he helped to clarify the reference. "The Optical Illusions Control Group is a company within a company, I suppose you could say. They dabble with the technological potentials of expansive virtual reality, whilst analyzing the impacts of that potential on members of society, as well as whole communities. If I am visualizing what you have just described having seen correctly, I can state, with reasonable certainty that the OIC Group are responsible for the colourful phenomenon that you have witnessed."

Miles followed the professor's explanation better than he suspected he was supposed to. "A company within a company, you say?" he asked. "Dare I assume that the parent company is, in fact, Quantus Enterprises?"

Professor Archaios smiled as if Miles were a particularly bright student. "Why, yes, that is quite correct."

Miles smiled back, "It seems there's one thing that is very much the same here, and where I am from," he mused. "Both societies have resorted to the abundant use of acronyms."

The Professor stared at Miles, almost appearing agitated at the suggestion of the Utopian society that he knew and loved having anything to do with a world that, while parallel, was decidedly quite different...and not necessarily in a good way.

Miles frowned as he saw signs of annoyance on Archaios' face. He chose to take a moment to check the time on his tablet. He looked back at the Professor as he realized that it was almost time for the professional wrestling event that was described in his research at the Library.

"Well, sir," Miles spoke up, wanting to change the subject and quickly try to appease his host and diffuse the situation. "There's an event happening at a place called the Konistra Coliseum. What is the best way for me to get there?" Miles watched as his host's face lit up with a sense of delight...or perhaps relief, at the thought that he had discovered some recreational activities that interested him.

"I recommend taking the sub-rail train." the Professor responded with a renewed enthusiasm. "There's a stop that connects directly to an entrance of the Coliseum; an idea beautifully inspired by the Montreal Metro System. When you first arrived, despite not being able to establish your identity, we *were* able to provide your DNA code with enough credits to allow you to get around, and find nourishment beyond that which we can provide in your room."

"Ahhh," Miles shared in the enthusiasm of the moment, but not for the same reasons. "I was quite surprised to find that the sub-rail system allowed me to pay a fare earlier by just my touch! That is quite the system that your world has developed, saves on resources and other expenses, I'll bet?"

"Indeed...indeed," the elderly gentleman nodded. A faint ringing stopped him as he started to lead the way to the door. Hesitantly, he turned towards Miles with a smile. "Sorry about that, it seems I am being called away. However, it sounds like I don't need to tell you how to get aboard the sub-rail from here, so I shall let you go to your event. I look forward to our next conversation, Mr. Militis."

"Thank you, Professor," Miles responded in kind. "Have yourself a good evening."

Once again, ensuring that he wasn't followed or being watched, Professor Olim Archaios accessed the concealed security area.

"What is your report? Have we determined where Mr. Militis was when we...when I called him?" The Professor asked the security officer who was looking over some statistical data.

"We have yet to pinpoint that information, Professor." The guard reported sternly. "But I was contacting you to find out if you wanted to adjust our approach to maintain a better focus and vigilance over his activities?"

"Hmmm," The Professor considered, and then shook his head. "No, he's only going to a wrestling event at the Coliseum this evening; let him enjoy his first night out."

Olim then pulled a recording device from his pocket and lay it on the desk in front of the officer. "I also want you to listen to this recording of the conversation that I've just had with him. It might do well for us to investigate the streak of colourful illumination that he described. That seems a bit beyond what the OIC Group tends to use for their purposes. Thankfully, he wasn't any the wiser about that." Olim instructed and then turned to help review the data on Miles' previous whereabouts himself.

CHAPTER 16

INVESTIGATIONS

HUMBER MEMORIAL HOSPITAL
TORONTO, ONTARIO
6:15am, Sunday, October 26th, 2014

After what seemed to be hours upon hours of waiting, and receiving no additional updates on the condition of his wife, Jack Erebus was growing quite impatient; his lack of decent sleep wasn't helping the situation. He had managed to close his eyes for 10-20 minutes here n there, but always woke up abruptly at the slightest sound of a voice; hoping that it would bring him news of Angelique's condition.

"We have some good news for you, Mr. Erebus." The attending physician declared, catching the preoccupied and fatigued visitor by surprise. Jack was relieved to finally see the doctor "Your wife has come out of her stupor, and regained a conscious state of awareness."

"That's great!" Jack was so excited, he interrupted the doctor. "When can I take her home?

"Well, this was a unique and serious case, Mr. Erebus." The

doctor replied with a frown. "We'd like her to remain in the hospital for the remainder of the day, and overnight, under close observation. As we do not know what caused this to occur, we can't guarantee she might not suffer a relapse."

Jack grumbled with disappointment, even though he knew in his heart of hearts that the doctor was right. After suffering through a long, noisy flight from Europe, and coming home to find his wife in an unresponsive condition, the last thing that he needed was to hear was that she'd have to spend more time in the hospital.

Frustrated, tired and disappointed, he visited briefly with Angelique, gave her a kiss on the forehead, and then left to return home.

☺☺☺

CENTRUS LABORATORIES:
RESEARCH LAB #2
7:07am, Sunday, October 26th, 2014

After having exhausted 3 full pots of coffee, Dr. Roger Thascalos and his young Asian apprentice Professor Eric Nidell struggled to continue their effort to acquire more information regarding the phenomenon that had taken place the previous evening.

Roger tried making a few calls to other departments, but it was too late at night, and all that he could do was leave some voicemail messages, and hope someone would get back to him.

Meanwhile, Eric was working at a feverish pace to try and discover the location of the occurrence.

"Have you learned anything more on these gravitational waves that you made reference to, or their alleged manipulation, and the impact of this potential?" Roger asked him.

"Nothing new has come up on that possibility," Eric replied sadly. "However, I've managed to pinpoint where the phenomenon took place. Perhaps we should take a closer look at the area?"

As he listened to his associate's response, Dr. Thascalos jumped at the chance to discover answers for himself. Motivated with hopes of perhaps detecting some localized readings, which might otherwise have been overlooked, the middle-aged scientist literally leapt off of the edge of the desk that he was leaning upon, and headed towards the door that led to a storage room.

"EXCELLENT!" Roger called out with a triumphant confidence. "I will grab a few things from storage so that we can work undisturbed. Get the car ready, and I will meet you out front."

Eric rose from his office chair and nodded politely, before turning to leave and follow the directions given by his superior.

🕐🕑🕒

SCIENTIFIC UNITY COMPLEX:
GUEST QUARTERS
7:02pm, Friday, November 23rd, 2018

Returning to his room, Miles approached the area of the wall where he'd originally received his clothes; hoping to find something a bit more casual, but stylish, for his night at the big event. Checking himself in the mirror, he really appreciated the variety of options this one closet managed to provide for him. Having made his selection, Miles turned towards the floating cot to consult the map, and see if he could locate a sub-rail terminal that was closer to his location than the first one he'd visited earlier. Taking a final look at himself in a reflective area of the wall by the door, he took a slow deep breath, and headed towards the exit.

CHAPTER 17

KONISTRA AND KARMA

The nearest sub rail station was actually located just around the corner. Shortly after stepping through the main door of the SUC, Miles turned the corner to find the entrance to the terminal near the rear of the oblong building. He descended the concrete steps towards the entrance gate swiftly, barely taking notice of the fact that the steps and the ground surrounding them were dissimilar from the surrounding grounds. With every other area that he'd explored so far, outside of Malum City, being perfectly clean and in order, he somehow did not observe the differences surrounding the area towards the rear of the Complex, and the nearby transit station. His mind was focused on the fact that his time was growing short before the wrestling event was scheduled to begin.

This Fares & Information kiosk differed slightly from the one that he had encountered earlier. Approaching the kiosk, the screen lit up and welcomed him to Synklisi Sub-Rail Station and simply asked him to press his thumb or finger against the pad to pay, and provided a "Help?" button for fare rate information.

Without hesitation, now knowing how the economics of this society worked…at least somewhat, he pressed his finger upon the pad and the gate opened in front of him. The train had arrived moments before, and he managed to get aboard just before it pulled away from the platform.

Looking around briefly, Miles decided to sit down this time and enjoy the smooth, quiet ride that this city's sub-rail transit system provided.

☺☺☺

QUANTUS ENTERPRISES:
GLIDER CONTROL ROOM
7:30pm, Friday, November 23rd, 2018

After having been left alone to observe the footage recorded by the Quantus Enterprises' glider, Anita O'Dell took the next step alone, and visited the unusual structure known as the Scientific Unity Complex. Even after having moved to Amgine City only a few short months ago, she was still a bit in awe of the Complex's unique exterior. She carefully walked around the oddly shaped structure, which looked decidedly out of place compared to the buildings that surrounded it. She pondered whether this was a significant fact that could lead to other answers down the road, but she realized that she wouldn't fully understand that, until the resolutions to her other queries were determined.

Finding no knob or handle on the door, she pushed against the main door of the Complex, which didn't budge, and then activated a pad on a communications panel to the right of the entrance. The panel lit up, and she heard a chime. "Scientific Unity Complex, Security Officer Murdoch speaking, please state your business" said a stern voice.

"My name is Anita O'Dell, and I am curious about this building and the recent goings on within. I wish to speak to someone in authority." The Irish accent was strong, but her voice was clear, as she replied to the disembodied voice. There was an extended pause and silence, as the security officer was likely checking with a superior regarding the inquiry. Finally, she heard a crackling noise and the voice spoke again.

"My apologies for the delay, Ms. O'Dell" the guard spoke politely. "However, we are unable to grant you access to the facilities of the Scientific Unity Complex at this time. We are under a partial lockdown, for the time being. We would welcome a written inquiry regarding your concerns, or you are invited to visit us again once the lockdown procedures have been cleared."

Anita frowned, her proactive efforts to assist with Administrator Thascalos' investigation were halted rather abruptly, and she was uncertain about how to proceed. Stepping back from the door, she thanked the guard, and turned towards the street. She knew better than to lurk around the door and raise suspicions or concerns on behalf of the security personnel inside the Complex. Looking down the street, her eyes fixed upon the tall building of the Main Library. If she couldn't visit the SUC, she could research it. She set off for the library.

۞۞۞

AMGINE CITY:
SUB-RAIL TRAIN, LINE 1, SOUTHBOUND
7:44pm, Friday, November 23rd, 2018

Miles felt unusually relaxed; the sub rail train moved so smoothly and quietly, a part of him wondered whether there might be something added to the ventilation system as well; something to invoke a sense of pacifism and ease perhaps.

The train finally arrived at his destination, not surprisingly it was named Konistra Station. Exiting the train, he found plenty of clearly written and colourful signage directing him towards the Coliseum entrance. Walking towards it, Miles reflected upon an earlier visit that he had once made to Montreal, Quebec, and his experience of the Metro subway system that had spanned the large city. He recalled finding the station leading to an underground entrance to the Olympic Stadium, and attending what was to be the Montreal Expos' second last baseball season "home opener" game.

Fascinated by these new surroundings that seemed to be so carefully designed to emulate those that he was once familiar with, Miles took his time appreciating some of the more intricate details of the style and craftsmanship. As it had been in the first sub-rail system that he had visited in Amgine City, everything down here was so...clean!

At the Konistra Coliseum ticket kiosk, Miles excitedly pressed his finger against the pad. It seemed to take an unusually long time to process his payment. Finally a screen lit up in front of him.

WELCOME TO THE KONISTRA COLISEUM!
We are pleased to inform you that
your arrival, and request for a ticket to our
special professional wrestling event, was well-timed.
We have had a cancellation from a regular guest
here at the Coliseum,
and their ticket is being provided to you, on their behalf.
There is no extra charge being applied
for this exclusive opportunity.
We hope that you enjoy the event and come to visit us again!

Shortly after the message ended, and the screen faded to black, a ticket was printed and provided to him on a small tray that protruded from the kiosk. Miles was absolutely dumbfounded to learn that his timing had somehow earned him a front row seat to the event!

Knowing there was very little time left, and excited by this sudden stroke of luck, Miles turned and power-walked towards the admissions portal. He was eager to see what the inside of the arena looked like, and whether he would be facing a side of the ring, or a ring corner, or whether he'd be near the entrance curtain/ramp.

Once inside the uniquely curved walls of the tunnel leading into the well-lit and rather large main section of the Coliseum, he stopped a moment to take it all in; taking a slow deep breath, imagining that he had just stepped through the curtain and was making his own way down towards the ring.

He asked a nearby hovering robot about his seat location. The automated usher led him to the front row and shone a directed beam of light over his seat. Once again marvelling at the technology that existed in this realm, Miles smiled as he sat down. Suddenly, he realized that he was seated near the table where the colour commentators were likely to be positioned; a discovery that made him all the more excited about what was to come!

It did not take long for the seats to fill, almost to capacity and for the show to begin. Miles was elated to have been right about his proximity to the colour commentators at ringside, but he *was* pleasantly surprised to find that this arena provided him with the option of using headsets to hear the commentary while watching the action.

Despite the advancements of technology, there were no robots involved in the actual matches, apart from the occasional robotic referee. The near-capacity crowd showed consistent spirited support for the matches, reminding him even more of that incredible Montreal Expos baseball game that he felt privileged to have seen live.

The wrestling card was impressive, and the commentary entertaining. Miles was most impressed with the variety of match types: a tag team match, a strap match, a cage match, even a good ol' fashioned lumberjack match. Despite his fascination with all that he had witnessed and experienced thus far, he was growing impatient for the main event, and seeing his ex-girlfriend's doppleganger in action.

CHAPTER 18

THE RING GODDESS

Finally the main event of the evening was due to start, and the back story was quite a tale. Miles listened carefully to the colour commentary as an incredibly vivid 3-D holographic presentation provided an edited rehashing of all that had taken place to bring the 2 superstars together; each segment having been projected directly over the ring in the center of the arena.

"The Canadian Wrestling Goddess had caught her #1 rival, the seductive and sadistic snake AshleyConda off guard by entering the ring during a televised event, and calling out her heated rival (and rumoured lover) to any one of a series of potential match types." The first commentator began. "Not being one to turn down such a challenge, the sneaky and somewhat superior Asian athlete rushed to the ring and signalled for a cage to be lowered. Ashley pressed right up against the outer perimeter of the ring, brimming with confidence, having accepted the challenge in the form of a steel cage match. It did not take long for these two legendary combatants to lock horns, and Ashley looked set to use every trick she could think of to make her blonde challenger wish that she had not issued the challenge."

"That's right, George!" The second commentator replied.

"And in the end, it was The Goddess herself who managed to turn the tables and put her #1 rival, and former tag partner, into a compromising and humiliating position. Faith managed to do so in a way that would send a message of her own, by applying AshleyConda's own finishing hold, a sleeper choke/body scissor combo, to put her opponent away!"

The impressive action being put on display, combined with the well-described commentary, almost prompted Miles to applaud at the reprisal of The Goddess' victory.

"Tensions reached a fever pitch last night when AshleyConda attempted to interfere in a singles match involving Goddess Faith's current tag team partner, The Black Widow." The first commentator continued, as the crowd groaned at the sight of what was being described. "Faith didn't take too kindly to this assault and attempted to cripple the Snake using a steel chair, but was fought off with a brutal low blow before AshleyConda slithered away into the shadows, vowing to return and have her revenge."

As the holograms faded, and the lights in the arena dimmed, the second commentator finished the lead-in with "Tonight is Ashley's first true chance at vengeance after that humiliating defeat in the cage. With the action ready to start, let's turn our attention to the present and see what unfolds."

A colourful display began lighting up a part of the arena, as a full set of fireworks exploded along the sides of the entrance ramp, up from the ringside floor towards the dais. Suddenly a lightning bolt zapped down from each of the four corners of the uniquely designed ceiling and erupted together at the top of the platform in a puff of smoke. Two search lights shone over the crowd briefly before focusing upon the gradually dissipating smoke, revealing the statuesque silhouette of the hometown favourite. The crowd started to go absolutely nuts as the lights slowly raised to their normal event level, and the "Goddess" made her way down the ramp with flair and confidence.

"Ladies and Gentlemen, the main event of the evening is a grudge match between the 2 top female wrestlers on the roster. Introducing first: from Amgine City, Ontario, Canada, standing at 5'8" tall, and weighing in this evening at a lean and lovely 132lbs, the Canadian Wrestling Goddess, FAITH!!!"

This evening, she was dressed to impress in her popular black French cut bikini and mid-calf black boots, which provided a stunning visual contrast between the bronze tan on her skin, and the golden blonde mane that flowed past her shoulders.

Cheers and applause were cut abruptly short, however, as The Goddess approached ringside, and was attacked from behind by her nemesis who was waiting in the shadows to pounce and gain her revenge.

Miles watched in horror as his ex-girlfriend's doppelganger ended up getting brutally attacked outside the ring before the bell could sound to start the match officially. The evil AshleyConda was dressed in a black and green catsuit, which hugged her own impressive figure, complete with a snake head lucha-style mask.

The action finally got brought into the ring, but what followed was a disappointment for the hometown fans, as the masked villainess used every trick she could to ensure her bold, beautiful blonde opponent could not hope to turn things around.

However, the snake got a bit too overzealous in her efforts, and assaulted the referee, which quickly earned her a disqualification. AshleyConda was livid, and she quickly pulled her blonde rival up off the mat, lifting her into the air and bringing Goddess Faith's beaten body crashing down across her knee in a backbreaker.

The intended message was clearly conveyed without a verbal exchange and the seductive snake slithered out of the ring. The fans and Faith knew for sure that the Snake was not going to let this rivalry end on a DQ. Another match would soon be scheduled.

Miles frowned as he watched the limp form of the Goddess lay on the mat, it only served to remind him of what he had lost. Amber and Faith shared a similar athletic stature and build, so the comparison was even more evident in person than in the library file.

With the event ending with such an unfortunate result, the crowd rose almost in unison and turned to leave. Miles remained patient for his chance to climb the stairs to the tunnel that would soon lead him back to the sub-rail terminal.

AMGINE CITY:
SUB-RAIL TRAIN, LINE 1, NORTHBOUND
11:11pm, Friday, November 23rd, 2018

Having wished for so long to have a 24 hour sub-rail service in his home town, Miles was quite relieved to find, despite the late hour, that he could still catch the train back to the comfort of his floating cot at the Scientific Unity Complex; though a part of him still wished that he was returning to the bedroom in Jack and Angelique's basement.

Approaching the SUC front entrance, he'd realized that he had no key or passcode or any instructions on how to gain entry.

"What if Olim is asleep or elsewhere?" he worried. Looking around the door and surrounding wall, he could not find the blue button that was present when he last returned to the building. Distracted by his inability to find a way to gain access, he failed to see another ripple of light cascade across the night sky, obscured by a few clouds, and by the unyielding darkness. Eyeing the communications pad, Miles pressed his finger upon it. Instead of the voice he'd been expecting, he heard a throbbing of energy as the door slid open. The communications panel must be an "off-hours" alternative to the blue button that he'd encountered on his previous return visit, Miles decided.

"Come right in, Mr. Militis, welcome back." The security officer's voice was unfamiliar to Miles, but he was just relieved to have gained access to the facility, and swiftly moved towards his designated room.

Stifling a yawn, Miles realized that a good night's sleep might help him to understand all that had taken place since the last time he laid down to rest; or, at least, the last time he did so intentionally. With fatigue quickly settling upon him, he reached the room that he was provided with by the Professor. It had been quite an emotionally and psychologically exhausting day. He collapsed effortlessly on the floating cot, and immediately succumbed to a deep sleep.

He didn't stay awake long enough to see the flashing purple light on the screen of his tablet. As he slumbered, he was unaware of the information that was being extracted from his tablet for study. Someone had found him out, and developed an interest in what he'd learned.

CHAPTER 19

CONFLICTS OF INTEREST

THE EREBUS RESIDENCE
8:00am, Sunday, October 26th, 2014

With his wife recovering and being kept at the hospital for further observation, Jack Erebus returned to his street to find that his property was surrounded by a barricade. Having parked by the curb, adjacent to the blockade, he wasted little time climbing out of his car and penetrating the perimeter to figure out what was going on. He was startled to discover 2 men in lab coats carefully observing the house.

"Excuse me, could one of you tell me what the hell is happening here?" Jack uttered, more brusquely than he had initially intended, as he approached the strangers.

Doctor Thascalos was caught off guard by the interruption to his investigative efforts; Professor Nidell seemed unphased, and continued to gather data about the property. The Doctor stopped looking around, and approached the new arrival.

"Good evening sir, I apologize if the security fence has inconvenienced you. I assure you, it is a necessary precaution.

Allow me to introduce myself. I am Doctor Roger Thascalos, and this is my..." the Doctor paused and noticed that his assistant was still working. Returning his attention to Jack, he smiled, "My dedicated and determined apprentice, Professor Eric Nidell. We've observed some strange readings in the vicinity of this property, and we are trying to investigate the source. We've been led to believe that something happened here during a particularly violent wind storm yesterday."

"*Something happened?*" Jack repeated questioningly, and then adjusted his tone. "Hmmm, well I am pleased to meet you gentlemen. My name is Jack Erebus, I am the owner of this property, and I am unaware of any..." Jack's voice trailed off, as the sky above them suddenly went black.

All three men looked up, startled by the abrupt change in lighting. Doctor Thascalos and Jack began looking around in a sudden panic of uncertainty, while Eric shrugged it off, and resumed his investigative efforts.

As the elemental darkness in the sky dissipated, Jack was ready to continue his dialogue with the Doctor, when he noticed something beyond Roger's shoulder, and his eyes widened in horror. He nervously pointed behind Doctor Thascalos at an area of the outer wall of the house that was still in need of repair, a part of the structure that Professor Nidell was gradually moving towards.

Realizing the danger, Thascalos cried out to his oblivious counterpart, "Eric! Look out!"

Eric recoiled from the swarm of spiders that were spilling out of an expanding hole in the wall. He was quick to realize that these were no ordinary spiders! Eric shone a light upon some of them, and their eyes appeared to reflect the light right back, but with a greater intensity, and an alternating spectrum of colours.

"Eric...ERIC! Get back from there, now!" the Doctor insisted, trying to prevent his assistant from being overrun by the mass amount of seemingly unusual arachnids that started enveloping the wall.

Jack didn't want to believe what he was seeing. He watched the seemingly hapless scientist being gradually surrounded by the eight-legged invaders, and brushed past Doctor Thascalos to try and rescue the young man. Charging in, Jack shoved Eric aside with a push hard enough to throw him clear of the swarm, which turned the attention of the mass of arachnids towards the rescuer. As Jack let out an agonizing yell that escalated into a somewhat metallic sounding roar, Eric jumped up and raced towards the barricade, with the Doctor on his heels.

"I think a strategic retreat is indicated here, Eric." Dr. Thascalos suggested, climbing partway into the driver's seat of their vehicle. But Eric had stopped at the perimeter of the fence, and returned his attention to the distracting sight of the new stranger being surrounded by the eight-legged mob. "DO AS I SAY!" Roger Thascalos barked, growing more demanding out of a combination of concern and frustration. "There is nothing we two can do from here. Those strange looking spiders seem to be staying close to the house, for now. We'll leave the barricade up to ward off others; hopefully nobody else will have to experience the fate that we have just witnessed that poor man suffer."

🕐🕑🕒

SCIENTIFIC UNITY COMPLEX
GUEST QUARTERS
8:36am, Saturday, November 24th, 2018

Miles awoke feeling very well rested and comfortable, which reminded him of the bed that he loved, and was laying on before this whole unusual adventure took place. He appreciated that this realm had aspects that he could compare with what he was accustomed to. However, despite the Professor's assurances, he was growing doubtful that he would ever truly learn how he came to be here, or why, or whether he would be able to make it back.

His first attempt to rise up to a seated position was met with hesitation; the combination of his enjoyment of the comfortable cot, and reflections of the previous evening causing him to want to just lay there and re-absorb everything. Staring up at the plain-looking ceiling, he re-envisioned the sight of his ex-girlfriend's unofficial clone...her doppelganger from this realm, showing off such incredible passion and athleticism. This would be the third time, since arriving in this dimension, which he would end up being reminded about his ex-girlfriend, but this time it felt more arousing than depressing. The unique facilities and amenities provided to patrons and guests of the Konistra Coliseum were absolutely staggering. The ability to see a holographic replay of action that led up to the main event, and the option of either being able to hear the commentary while watching the action or just soak in the live entertainment and all of its facets was truly worthy of remembrance.

He sighed. At some point, he knew that he would have to try to get up again. He grabbed the tablet to check for the weather forecast. While he had hoped to learn more about the world around him, he was disappointed to read about the overcast weather report. He was glad it wasn't supposed to rain and it felt odd, almost surreal. Reading such a forecast and knowing that he could trust it to be accurate.

He rolled to the edge of the floating cot and accessed the wall panel that had given him breakfast the day before. He wondered whether the system really could somehow read his thoughts, or if it would just identify and provide what he had last consumed. He concentrated on a personal favourite, and pressed the glowing portion of the panel. Once again, the wall hummed and groaned before one part of it became transparent and slid aside. There, presented in front of him, to his pleasure, was one of the nicest looking omelettes he'd ever seen. It smelled wonderful, and actually made his mouth water at the thought of its taste. He reached in carefully for the plate and cutlery, and turned to find the table and chair there waiting for him. This place had become his new home, and it seemed to be warming to him as quickly as he was adapting to his new environment.

An unfamiliar ringing sound interrupted the silence in the relatively empty room, the noise was emanating from his tablet on the cot. He approached the computer to find a familiar icon flashing upon it. Clearly this tablet was pre-designed to use different tones for different contacts. He eagerly pressed the flashing icon, wondering who it might be that was calling him this time, and why?

"Hello, Mr. Militis, it's Velvet," the softly accented voice emanated clearly from the speaker. "I was wondering if you were interested in grabbing some food later. I know of a great restaurant in town that I think you would enjoy."

Miles' face lit up with the thought that Velvet wanted to see him to the extent of calling him out for a date. "*A woman is asking a man out? That is something that almost NEVER happens on MY Earth!*" he thought to himself before realizing that he had left his new friend waiting for his response.

"Good morning, Velvet. Yes, that does sound like an enticing invitation. It would give us the opportunity to meet up without bumping into each other...unexpectedly." Miles teased remembering their previous 2 encounters during his time in the city. "I'm just about to sit down to breakfast, and plan my day. But I will call you later to determine when and where we can meet to have this meal."

A soft purr could be heard from the speaker on the tablet before Velvet confirmed the suggestion and politely ended the conversation.

☺☺☺

CENTRUS LABORATORIES: EXPERIMENTAL SCIENCES DEPARTMENT
8:28am, Sunday, October 26th, 2014

Meanwhile, in the dimly lit control room, while trying to improve upon the initial test run of his experiment, Lupo heard another alarm, and the security monitor's screen showed him Jack Erebus's unfortunate fate. Lupo growled and moaned as if in agony as Erebus was overtaken and absorbed by the swarm of unusual spiders. The suddenly troubled and distorted figure of Lupo uttered an ear-piercing shriek that filled the large empty room. The high-pitched sound seemed to last a good 5 minutes, but by the time someone else opened the door to investigate, the cloaked figure of Lupo had disappeared, and only his cloak remained!

☺☺☺

AMGINE CITY:
DOWNTOWN
4:39pm, Saturday, November 24th, 2018

At the intersection across from the Library, Mikes patiently waited for the light to change, then crossed the street and re-entered the magnificently designed Amgine City Main Library. This beautiful building was becoming quite a welcoming place to him, much like his new temporary "room and board" accommodations. He boarded the elevator and asked for the 4th floor. It was kind of a sweet and kinky idea for Velvet to suggest meeting where they had, quite literally, bumped into each other the first time.

Finding a comfortable chair, he relaxed for a few minutes. Velvet didn't keep him waiting very long though, as she appeared in a stunning, form-fitting black leather outfit, with black fishnet hose leading to a pair of mid-calf black leather boots.

"Hello Miles, fancy meeting you here." Velvet greeted him with a soft giggle and a wry grin. Taking a quick look around at her surroundings, as if she did not often spend much time in the Library, she gestured towards the elevators. "Shall we get going?"

Miles nodded and then watched as she turned towards the elevator, and lunged for the button to stop the elevator car from going back down without them. Miles sighed softly and sadly, the smile that had appeared across his lips faded swiftly as a part of him just wanted to just break down and fall to his knees crying. As she turned to face him and wait for him to join her, he struggled to maintain his composure. Being in the presence of such a beautiful, confident woman naturally reminded him of his ex-girlfriend, and it made him wonder about what had happened to his dear friend Angelique after he suddenly disappeared?

CHAPTER 20

REVELATIONS

HUMBER MEMORIAL HOSPITAL
10:05am, Sunday, October 26th, 2014

After having finally been cleared by the physicians, Angelique Lambros-Erebus was eager to leave the hospital, and try to make sense of what all had transpired. Despite having promised the Doctor that she would "take it easy for a few days", she felt determined to learn more about the events that led to her being hospitalized. She stopped at the exit, and then pulled out her cellphone to call home. It rang a half dozen times then went to the answering machine. Angelique was perplexed, and naturally concerned, wondering where her husband Jack was. Her biggest nagging fear that she could not seem to shake was that he too had disappeared, just like their friend Miles seemed to have.

"Miles..." she whispered under her breath as she redialled her cell phone again and again, with no change in the results. She frowned, looking around the hospital grounds, wondering how to get home. She pulled out an emergency $50 that she had stashed in a secret compartment in her purse, headed towards the curb, and hailed a taxi.

☺☺☺

AMGINE CITY:
MAIN LIBRARY
4:55pm, Saturday, November 24th, 2018

Letting his determined companion take the initiative, Miles enjoyed the scenery while Velvet drove him towards her chosen restaurant. She turned into an awkwardly angled driveway leading to a rather uniquely well-designed parking lot outside of Giovanni's Pizza Palace. The parking lot and exterior of the restaurant were designed to emulate aspects of a true Italian experience. They were stopped by a shuttle bus which looked very much like a Venetian Canal gondola, taking the ambience even further. Velvet appeared to be very selective about where she wanted to park, no doubt wishing to avoid the possibility of her vehicle drawing undue attention from any law enforcement personnel.

"Follow my lead," Velvet purred, while looking at her passenger with a sultry gaze. Miles had no reason, nor any compulsion, to decline her request and complied. He couldn't help but admire her physique once again, but now focussing on the swivel of her narrow hips.

The interior of the restaurant seemed quite vast, compared to how small it had appeared from the outside. Miles noticed that it looked to be a reasonably quiet evening inside the restaurant, and that the greeter seemed to recognize Velvet and led them to a very quiet, private table. Allowing Velvet to choose which side she wanted to sit, he watched those long lovely legs bend and slip under the table, before he caught himself staring at them, and taking his own seat across from her.

Velvet observed his admiring gaze and smiled. She purred softly, stopping Miles from grabbing his menu, her soft hand laid somewhat firmly upon his, as their eyes locked across the table.

"Do you trust me?" she asked softly.

Miles shivered a bit from the sudden feel of her hand, blocking his attempt to look at the menu. Getting lost in her eyes for only a mere half second, he nodded slowly.

"Yes, of course. You do seem to be known here, so obviously the menu must be relatively familiar to you...surprise me!" he replied, attempting to appear confident.

With a beaming smile, the lady directed her attention to the waiter.

"I'll have my usual, but make it a large, and could you please add a side order of garlic cheese bread?" Velvet rhymed off the order with ease and confidence.

The waiter silently nodded and politely moved to turn away to check on his other tables.

"And a bottle of Argentina Malbec," Miles called after him, suddenly realizing he didn't know what year would be a good one to choose in this realm. "The best one that you have." he finished. The waiter nodded again, and turned to walk away to catch the attention of the Sommelier, for the wine order.

Pushing the menus aside, stifling a bit of a laugh that the waiter had left them behind, Miles turned his other hand around to hold Velvet's, as their eyes locked once again.

"Of all the wonders that I have seen since arriving here," Miles started, feeling particularly bold and flirty. "You are definitely one of the more alluring, and fascinating ones." His eyes suddenly widened a little, remembering the magnificent sights that he had just witnessed at the Konistra Coliseum, but he laboured to maintain a look of sincerity, despite the thoughts that had entered his mind at that particular moment.

Velvet could feel her cheeks starting to redden from the flattering words of her dinner companion. However, his facial expression shifted and his gaze unfocused momentarily, making her wonder why. The Sommelier's arrival at the table with the bottle of Argentinean Malbec was timely enough to snap him out of his stupor.

"Mmmm, it's just amazing how great each experience that I have had, since coming to Amgine City, has been. I am, naturally, very pleased and impressed with the people whom I have met so far, as well." Miles smiled brightly, his voice once again brimming with flirty confidence. "If you have not tried a Malbec wine yet, you are in for a treat, and if you have...then I look forward to learning about what other things we share in common with one another."

Watching the Sommelier pour the wine, after having been provided with a small sampling to ensure his satisfaction, Miles eagerly reached forward to hand Velvet her glass, raising his in a toasting gesture. "Here's to a delicious meal and stimulating conversation."

Velvet raised her glass to clink with his, and took a sip of the crimson nectar. Hesitantly, she pulled the glass away from her lips, and gazed at it carefully, before quickly taking another sip.

"You certainly were not wrong, Miles." she lamented. "This is a very, very nice wine indeed." Hearing his words ring through her mind, she leaned back in her chair to get comfortable. "So, tell me about what you have been up to since I saw you last, Miles."

"Well, I took in some fascinating entertainment last night." Miles opted to share his most recent and by far most enjoyable experience since his adventure in Malum City. "I learned about this professional wrestling event being held at the Konistra Coliseum during my initial researches at the Library." He paused, giving his dinner companion a hinting wink. "Which is when you and I first…"met", hehe." Miles used air quotes to indicate the sarcastic use of the word, and watched as Velvet joined in his gleeful reflection on their first encounter at the Library.

He struggled to continue his story, as he felt her playfully brush her foot along his calf under the table, but then watched her lean forward to listen intently.

"Anyway," Miles cleared his throat after squirming a bit from the distracting feel of her foot against his leg. "I was rather taken aback to see an image of the Women's Wrestling Champion. She looks SO much like my ex-girlfriend, Amber, that I needed to see her in person. Her real name is Krystal Knight, at least here it is, but her ring name is…"

"The Canadian Wrestling Goddess…" Velvet interrupted, finishing the sentence for him. With an impassioned sigh, she removed her foot from his leg as she finished his sentence. "Faith…" Her eyes narrowed as she stared off into space, beyond Miles' left shoulder; a sad twinkle was evident in her gorgeously exotic eyes.

The awkward silence that followed told Miles that he had hit a nerve.

"I ummm…" at first, unsure how else to proceed, Miles was determined to continue, but he fumbled in his efforts to resume his anecdote. A few moments later, he tried again but although he opened his mouth, he could not utter a sound, arrested by the sad silence from his companion. "Sooo--I am guessing you two ladies are acquainted?" Miles tried to alter his approach to see if he could learn more about Velvet, Goddess Faith, and the as yet undefined emotion that Velvet felt towards the incredible blonde wrestler.

Velvet didn't respond immediately, preoccupied by what were, from her expression, strong conflicting emotions towards the "Goddess."

"Yes…you could say that," she finally answered his question. "Before I became a part of Josef's team, she was my tag team partner…and my lover."

Miles couldn't help but imagine these 2 lovely ladies together, biting his bottom lip to stop himself from responding with something off-the-wall like *"Well, I guess that means we share a similar taste in women too!"* Instead, he went for a more tactful approach.

"Well, if you'd rather not talk about it," Miles started carefully. "I won't push, though I will admit to being intrigued."

"Thank you, Miles," Velvet sighed after remaining still for a few more moments. "But I think there will be other, more appropriate times to cover that particular subject. I cannot deny my surprise and curiosity at the thought of another woman like her existing in...well, wherever it is that you came from. I'm guessing there are other people who have a similar appearance, between the two realms. Not quite clones, of course. But..." she paused again, "Sorry, I'm rambling. Tell me more about this Amber and life in that other realm of yours."

Miles didn't mind her "rambling" one bit, he loved her accent, and it only helped to enhance the incredible imagery of the idea that Velvet and Faith were teamed up together in the ring...and the bedroom.

"Oh, hmmm...well, Amber was..." fumbling over his words again, Miles wished she hadn't declined to go into detail about her ex and start asking about his. He took a few moments to compose himself, took a deep breath, and attempted to think of a different approach. Reaching for a glass of wine, he stalled for a few more minutes before elaborating on life in his home realm.

With their focus on each other, as they struggled through this awkward moment, they remained unaware of a pair of figures standing in the shadows outside the restaurant. They were being watched!

CHAPTER 21

SUSPICIONS

CENTRUS LABORATORIES:
RESEARCH LAB #2
10:11am, Sunday, October 26th, 2014

Both Thascalos and Nidell remained silent, as they returned to their laboratory; their eyes and facial expressions not having changed much since witnessing what took place at the Erebus household. Eric fell back into his chair struggling to make his eyes focus on the screen in front of him. After a few minutes, he slammed his palm down upon the desk, and shoved his rolling office chair back from it, throwing his head back with a grunt of disgust.

"We should've done *something...*" the younger man said with a sigh.

"That's the most emotion that I have seen you express since we started working together, Eric." The Doctor mused, but his apprentice's stunned, almost panicked, expression did not change from when they encountered the swarm of uncommon spiders pouring out from the side of the Erebus residence.

Taking a slow deep breath, Thascalos looked to his colleague and tried a more supportive approach. "There was nothing that we could've done for him, at least not at the time. The best thing we can truly do for him now is to try to find out where those spiders came from, how long they have been there, and how they might relate to other events that have taken place in that area of late."

Nidell heard the calmly presented logic, and was not oblivious to the odd and likely temporary role reversal that seemed to have taken place between himself and the Doctor. He considered Roger's words carefully; a part of him was still getting over nearly being overrun by the monstrous swarm of unusual arachnids. Against his own better judgment and comfort level, he forced himself to think back to the events that they had just witnessed and experienced. Within mere moments he sat upright, his mouth agape, as his reflection on the event helped him recall something potentially important.

"Those...those...spiders..." Eric hesitantly started; his voice a bit shaky. "There was something odd about them." He paused, his face showing a mix of fear, confusion, and revulsion. "*Their eyes,* oh my goodness, of course, I shone my flashlight at them, and their eyes seemed to absorb the light, and reflect it back...but it looked like the light in their eyes was...was brighter and actually changed colours!" Looking more confident and determined, he swiftly moved back to his computer terminal. "That characteristic might hold a clue, if I can just find the right breed."

Roger Thascalos observed his associate carefully, evaluating Eric's words, and the sudden epiphany. He could only replay the sight and sound of the home owner, Mr. Erebus, being absorbed by that mob of arachnids. Admiring the determination that Eric was showing in trying to research what kind of spider they had encountered. With a calming deep breath, he realized it would just be a matter of time before they could find more of the answers that they needed in order to put this grand and complicated puzzle together.

"Time…" he pondered to himself. *"Will we have enough time?"*

☉☉☉

AMGINE CITY:
GIOVANNI'S PIZZA PALACE
7:02pm, Saturday, November 24th, 2018

"Well, all 4 of my grandparents died by the time I was 32," Miles recalled, as it was his turn to share his own family history. "Some of my friends were more fortunate to have grandparents into their 40s'; others lost their parents before they were 20. It really is a mess where I come from. Which made the information that I learned at the Amgine City Library all the more incredible to me, particularly after hearing about the Century Life Mandate." Miles paused to take a sip of his excellent wine, taking a moment to catch Velvet's gaze, and observe the frown that formed on her face. "What's wrong?"

"I guess I've just gotten so accustomed to how things are here," She started, sniffling a bit as she shook her head in disbelief. "I cannot imagine that there's another Earth where people die so needlessly to common diseases…and then there's the violence!"

This time it was Miles' turn to hold her hand, and their eyes locked once more. Despite her reaction to the subject, and where the conversation led, Miles was determined to continue; hoping to help her understand one of the most important reasons as to why things were so different.

"I remember specifically when it was discovered that the scientists in my realm could use cloning to enhance medical research," He resumed from where he had left off. "But, unfortunately, my world wasn't quite so lucky when it came to the "moral", but often strongly religious, upheaval that followed." He took another pause, needing a few sips of wine for this final revelation. "A lot of good, decent people have died needlessly early as a result of people in power folding to the forces of activism that stood against the potential use of cloning in that manner." He stared vacantly at his glass, his eyes revealing the deep sadness within.

Miles' momentary trance-like state was interrupted by the approach of the waiter.

"Ms. Velvet, I regret to inform you that we have had some difficulties in the kitchen this evening." The waiter explained. "We are working to re-create your pizza from scratch. For this extended delay, however, there will be no charge for this meal.

"Well…" Miles said wryly, waiting for the waiter to be out of earshot. "I guess not *everything* is so different."

"Seems quite a lot of things are," Velvet said. "It sounds like we have more time than I thought." She reached towards Miles' tablet. "May I?" Miles nodded and slid his tablet toward her. "You were telling me about your fascination with history," she said, "and where things originated, including that story about pizza not having become a recognized thing until the 18th century." Velvet started browsing the tablet's applications.

"Yes," Miles replied. "I had just started reading about how different foods, and other everyday items, were first introduced to the world. My best friend's husband, Jack, kind of inspired my interest. He is big on Greek history and philosophy, but also a bit of a future tech guru as well. I mean, some just assume that food is there and that's what's important, but sometimes I find it fun to go deeper than that." He paused, seeing the words "Quantus Historical Database" on the screen. It quickly became apparent to him that he spent so much time exploring his new surroundings, and getting into some adventures in the process; that he didn't take the time to realize that the tablet which Professor Archaios had provided him with was more than just a map reader and communications device. It was a much more versatile piece of technology.

As it looked like Velvet was about ready to show him what she was looking for, he finished his thought. "Being in a pizza restaurant, I recalled one of my more recent researches into the history of how pizza came to be...at least, where it originated here, in my world."

Velvet navigated the operating system expertly, and it did not take her long to find the information that she wanted. Turning the tablet to face Miles, she allowed him to read the history of the pizza in this reality. His eyes widened in shock to learn that it was, in fact, introduced to settle one of the final arguments regarding the spherical nature of the planet. The man who owned the cheese stand, that a young Christopher Columbus would eventually work at, was credited with first introducing the now-popular Italian food. Once it was clear that Miles had finished reading over the data, Velvet spoke again.

"There is a video re-enactment of the event," she said while pressing the tablet flat upon the table. She then pressed a button on the tablet to run the media file. A holographic video display formed across the full length of the screen, causing Miles to lean back a bit. He watched as 2 angry mobs appeared in the simulation, coming together in the center of a market square; the leader of each side stepping forward on their own to confront each other with their argument.

"The world, she's a-flat!" claimed the first gentleman.

"No-no-no-no, the world, she's a-round!" the other man argued. The combined mass of humanity grew increasingly unsettled as this argument continued to go nowhere.

"Wait, wait, wait...I have something of a solution for you a-both, and can make enough for-a you all!" The short Italian man, clearly dressed as a baker stepped between the opposing sides, and lifted the lid on a steaming piece of flatbread with melted cheese and tomato sauce upon it. "It's-a my new creation, I call it a pizza. You see? It's-a both a-flat...*AND* it's a-round!" The simulation ceased a few moments after the presentation of the first pizza, and the holographic image vanished.

Miles stared agape at what he had just witnessed. He had doubts about the validity of what was presented to him, but tried to remind himself that it was a re-enactment, and that nobody would really be able to identify how one Italian baker who owned a cheese stand would come to help keep the tempers cooled, and inspire the great explorer Christopher Columbus to set out and prove that the world was indeed round, and traversable.

"Of course, the re-enactment was done to make history more enticing for the younger generations," Velvet broke the silence between them finally. "So, it's bound to be a bit more entertaining than how it actually occurred."

Miles smiled and nodded, but as he reached to turn the tablet off, his hand was once again stopped by hers. The flashing purple light in the corner of the screen, that Miles had remained ignorant of up to that point, had suddenly caught Velvet's attention.

"Wait!" she barked insistently, glaring down at the light, then up at Miles, then back down at the tablet. "Wait a goddamn minute! Wha--what the..." she glared back into Miles' eyes with bewilderment. "What the hell?" She looked around in a somewhat panicky sort of way, pushed her way out of the booth, brushing past the approaching waiter, and headed swiftly towards the exit.

Miles sat stunned after his companion left without so much as a "goodbye", while the odd purple icon in a corner of the tablet screen still continued to flash. He waved for the somewhat startled waiter while he looked to see what the purple light might signify, but could find nothing referring to it or what might prompt its appearance. Finally, caught the waiter's attention, intent on paying the bill, only to recall that they didn't actually get the chance to eat. The waiter approached and Miles cancelled their order. The waiter then informed him that there would be no charge for the wine, due to the issues with the originally ordered meal. Thanking him, and apologizing politely, Miles turned to leave. Moving hurriedly towards the exit, Miles hoped that he could still catch up with Velvet before she drove off.

Rushing into the parking lot, however, he nearly knocked down a blind woman approaching the curb at the corner. Having tripped over her walking stick, he managed to help her regain her balance, and subsequently his own. Stepping back and getting a better look at her, he was surprised to find that her form and some facial features seemed oddly recognizable.

"I'm very, very sorry, Miss." Miles apologized. "I really

should've been more careful …ummm. Please accept my apologies, would you like some help getting across the street?"

"Oh dear, uhhh yes, I suppose that really is the least that you could do after nearly running me over." The woman's voice was soft, somewhat familiar, and had a hint of levity to it.

Miles smiled at her tongue-in-cheek manner, and sighed with relief. Guiding her to the corner curb, he waited for the signals to change as the path before them became well-lit, and he led her to the other side.

"There now, guess my being here, when I was, turned out to be lucky after all, eh?" Miles quipped, attempting to respond to her jovial remark.

The woman reset her stick and smiled, then realized that her new acquaintance might be turning to leave, and let her stick slip out from under her so she stumbled towards the wall of the building that they were standing in front of.

Miles lunged and caught hold of her once again to help her regain her balance. She smiled at him, and he returned the smile, realizing belatedly that she might not be able to see it.

The woman still seemed unsteady, and let out a cough. Leaning against the wall for support and to get her bearings, she then began silently pointing and gesturing around the near corner of the building in front of them. Miles understood that she wanted him to help her to her indicated destination.

The side street that they had turned towards was rather poorly lit, when compared to what Miles had already seen of Amgine City. He moved carefully, ensuring that his new companion was kept stable on her feet every step of the way. But, once they passed the first building and crossed in front of the alley to the next, Miles was suddenly struck bluntly from behind, and collapsed in the shadow of the shrouded figure that stepped out from the darkness of the alley.

"Now, Miles, my old friend," Grylos hissed. "We clearly have a lot to talk about. No doubt we have some catching up to do, and more importantly we shall perhaps find out how you came to be here...and why!"

CHAPTER 22

CONCLUSIVE EVIDENCE

HUMBER MEMORIAL HOSPITAL
10:27am, Sunday, October 26th, 2014

It seemed to take forever for Angelique Lambros-Erebus to attract the attention of an available taxi. Finally waving one down, she gave the driver her address, presenting one of her husband's business cards for clarification. The cabbie nodded, pulled the flag down, and proceeded to drive towards the address indicated.

Staring out of the window, still trying to make sense of everything that she'd experienced over the course of the past few days. She still had no idea what had become of Miles, nor why she could not reach Jack on the phone. She fought against her natural urge to assume the worst, in both cases, and did her best to wait and see what she would discover when she finally got home.

As the taxi arrived on her street, the driver slowed his vehicle as it approached the barricade that was still in place; coasting past the opening and coming to an abrupt halt. Handing the cab driver the $50 that she had pulled out from the emergency compartment in her purse, Angelique took the change and left a tip so generous that the driver wondered if she had been paying enough attention to what she was doing.

Angelique saw the security fencing surrounding much of the property, but she could see no other people, nor any signs that indicated why the house was being blocked off. As she approached the house, her eyes were drawn to a glowing light source emanating from a hole in the wall; a hole she could have sworn was a smaller size the last time she had seen it. As she drew nearer, the illumination faded. Frustrated, she moved towards the side door of the house at a quicker pace, fumbling in her purse for the key.

Pushing her way inside, she saw Jack's luggage by the door, confirming that he had indeed returned; an observation that prompted a mix of relief and concern to build within her.

"Jack?" She called out, "You home? Miles? Are you here?" She continued to call them, but received no answer as she slowly searched the premises. She opened the door to the basement, and observed a similar light coming from the spare bedroom. "Miles?" she yelled once more, to no response.

Taking a slow deep breath, trying to calm her anxiety from this eerily uncertain situation, she slowly descended the stairs towards the glowing spare bedroom.

MALUM CITY:
DEPRAVUS TOWER
8:52pm, Saturday, November 24th, 2018

Josef Aros frowned as Velvet reported on what had occurred during her date with Miles Militis.

"I'm not sure what is really going on," Velvet relented, "But I feel, and fear, that there may be more to Miles than we realized. That flashing purple icon on his tablet was clearly a signal from a tracking device of some kind. If he was..." she paused, her face twisting in disgust. "UGHHH! I don't even want to think about it!"

"You suspect him of something malicious?" Josef asked.

"Is it possible that we could have been so blind?" Velvet replied. "Could Miles have played the ideal patsy, and the perfect bait, for us to reveal ourselves to our enemies? Could he have, somehow, allowed himself to be captured by us..." she swallowed, "...by me?"

Josef rose from his chair, troubled by his loyal counterpart's doubts about their judgement taking Miles into their confidence and allowing him involvement in their operations. Pacing slowly around the room, gazing out of a darkly tinted window, he finally turned back towards his distraught companion, near-missing the sight of another cascading line of colour streaming across the sky outside the window that he had just been staring at.

"Velvet, you know that I have been around for a lot of years. I have met a lot of people, and I've learned how to read them. I'm a pretty good judge of character, and an excellent judge of when I'm being lied to. I cannot bring myself around to the idea that Miles is involved in any plot to expose us, nor harm us. I do respect the conclusions that you've drawn, based on the evidence at hand. But, I am convinced that there must be some other answer."

Velvet leaned back in her recliner, trying to calm herself with the combination of its soft cushioning and Josef's words. She began to realize that she could be totally misinterpreting what she'd seen.

"What about that tracking device?" Velvet queried speculatively. "If it's true that's what it was…"

"If it's true, then Miles may be in grave danger," Josef interrupted, "And potentially in desperate need of our help…"

☺☺☺

QUANTUS ENTERPRISES:
LOBOS CHAMBER #314
9:38pm, Saturday, November 24th, 2018

Grylos paced impatiently inside a darkened room, the only light source in the room was carefully focused upon the surgical table, where an unconscious Miles Militis lay.

"Giatros had better get here soon…" he muttered with a growl at his visually impaired, blonde assistant. "I want to know what is on that tablet, and perhaps he can also help me get answers from my old friend here, who now lies peacefully prone." The agitated, cybernetically-enhanced figure then gestured to another figure that was chained to the nearby wall. The gesture triggered an automatic lighting mechanism which illuminated the limply hanging body of Anita O'Dell! "And then we can find out what this one knows as well!"

Giatros O. Opoios was a world renowned scientific advisor to the Quantus Enterprises. There were some technical details in the development of the security software on Miles' device that made it difficult, in fact nearly impossible, for Grylos and his assistant to access the information on it by any means; including the use of the mobile tracker, and direct manipulation.

There was a knock at the door, and Grylos anxiously brushed past his assistant to reach the door first and opened it, expecting Giatros, but instead finding Administrator Peter Thascalos.

Taking a half step in, Peter Thascalos looked just beyond Grylos' bulbous form, as his eyes were quickly directed first towards the unexpected appearance of his unconscious young assistant, Anita O'Dell hanging from shackles in the most distant part of the room. Relieved to see that she appeared unharmed, Peter's eyes then focused on the more anticipated and familiar sight of Miles Militis; who was lying motionless on a surgical table of sorts. His eyes shifted between both motionless figures before he narrowed his gaze into the partly glowing eyes of Grylos.

"It would appear," Thascalos started, "that we have much to talk about, you and I."

CHAPTER 23

CAUSE AND EFFECT

CENTRUS LABORATORIES:
RESEARCH LAB #2
12:38pm, Sunday, October 26th, 2014

While Eric Nidell went back to his trusty computer terminal to find answers, Doctor Thascalos heard the phone ring and was quick to answer it.

"Roger Thascalos." He answered, in his usual formal tone. His eyes widening as the voice on the other end described events that had apparently taken place elsewhere in the building. "Lupo's gone? Quantubus what? But…Alright, alright, no need to quote the operating procedures at me, I'll come." He swiftly hung up the phone and turned to his hardworking assistant. "I need to head down to the Experimental Sciences Department; something's happened down there…someone's disappeared."

Not waiting to be acknowledged by Eric, Roger headed quickly for the door.

"*I'VE GOT IT!*" Eric shouted excitedly, to nobody. "I should've realized before, those things must've been Wolf Spiders,

147

or some variation of that species." Spinning in his chair, he was shocked to learn that he was actually alone in the room. "Roger?"

Scratching his chin thoughtfully, Eric shrugged and returned to his research efforts. Now that he'd determined the probable breed of the spiders that had attacked him and Jack Erebus, he still wanted to know why they were there, and in such vast numbers!

QUANTUS ENTERPRISES: LOBOS CHAMBER #314
10:55pm, Saturday, November 24th, 2018

Grylos' glowing eyes shone a bright shade of red, which was either as a sign of intimidation towards his unwelcome guest, or a means of identifying that he was feeling angry. Grylos growled and turned away from the door, waving his metallic arm around in a gesture directing Administrator Peter Thascalos to enter the room.

"I am uncertain at this time that we need to have any dialogue, Thascalos!" Grylos grumbled, wondering what was keeping his originally anticipated guest Giatros.

"Well, we can start," Peter wasted little time starting his intended discussion. "With why you have my assistant chained to a wall and have this fellow laid out on a table."

With a growl of annoyance, Grylos pointed swiftly at the limply hanging, pale-skinned figure of Anita O'Dell first. "*She* started poking her nose into things that would've made her a threat to my project and related efforts." He then moved towards Miles, who lay prone on the surgical table. "And this man is known to me...but not in this realm. He shouldn't be here, he is an anomaly that needs to be investigated and potentially purged."

"*Purged?*" Administrator Thascalos repeated in utter shock of such a word being used to refer to the handling of a human being. "Grylos, I understand that you are in pain, angry, and determined to find a way to reverse what has been done to you. But I cannot allow you to misappropriate and misuse Quantus Enterprises facilities to aid in the elimination of a living human being; particularly one who has, so far, not done us any harm."

The Administrator then diverted his attention towards the lovely figure of his short-term assistant Anita O'Dell. "I don't know what she was investigating specifically, or why, or how you felt it would be a threat to your work; but I'm at least relieved that you don't seem to have similar...malicious...intentions..." The Administrator's words slowed as he heard some unusual noises that caused his empowered tirade to end prematurely. Peter Thascalos turned to face the figure who provoked his rage, his eyes widening at what he was observing, "G-G-Grylos?"

Grylos shook as he collapsed against a computer console. It was clearly not the words that were being uttered by his unexpected guest that were affecting him, but something else, something unseen. Using what little control he had left over his body, he growled and swung his arm back towards the door, trying to direct Administrator Thascalos back towards the door. But Peter Thascalos didn't move, his eyes filled with shock and horror as he witnessed his once proud and powerful, if unusual, fellow scientist slump to the floor where he writhed and twisted violently before vanishing completely.

Peter Thascalos stared in blank astonishment at the space where Grylos had disappeared from, without even a puff of smoke or any residue left behind. He then turned and hurried to free Anita from her shackles, carefully lowering her to a comfortable chair that was positioned nearby. Checking her pulse, and making sure that she was positioned in a reasonably comfortable and dignified manner, he turned his attention to Miles; not having realized that Grylos' visually-impaired assistant was also silently suffering. She had entered the room quietly from a concealed compartment, and struggled to find her way towards the exit.

The trembling figure of Grylos' assistant finally slumped to the floor, and just before disappearing, she could barely be heard uttering out "Miles…"

SCIENTIFIC UNITY COMPLEX: SECURITY CHAMBER K-1
11:33pm, Saturday, November 24th, 2018

Professor Olim Archaios was at a loss to explain the sudden disappearance of Miles Militis. But he was not given much time to try and figure out what had happened to his guest, as a klaxon sounded and drew his attention to a specially designed, but seldom used tracking system. Looking at the data that was appearing on the screen he could not believe what he was seeing.

"The Quantubus Effect?" he read to himself aloud, "Again?" Dashing towards a different computer terminal, he started punching up some historical information that, he hoped, would help him figure out how to proceed.

☺☺☺

CENTRUS LABORATORIES: EXPERIMENTAL SCIENCES DEPARTMENT
1:01pm, Sunday, October 26th, 2014

Roger Thascalos carefully pushed open the main door to the Experimental Sciences Department and peered in to see a great deal of activity taking place. The head of the department, Mr. Marcus Peirama, approached him.

"Thank you so much for coming down, Roger." Peirama greeted his fellow scientist warmly, despite the panic and uncertainty in the air. Sometimes Marcus felt it was best to take things in stride. "As you can see, there's quite a hubbub down here. One of our physicists, Lupo, has disappeared inexplicably."

"Disappeared?" Dr. Thascalos repeated curiously. "Who was he? And where was he last seen?"

"Lupo was our top experimental physicist," Marcus started. "He was a bit of an odd case, a hermit, and there was something about him...something about his eyes." Pointing towards a doorway behind the Doctor's right shoulder, he directed the elder scientist's attention to the room where Lupo was last seen. A tall security guard of average build stood guard of the entrance, who nodded at Marcus' signal. "He almost always worked, ate, and slept in his specially-designed laboratory."

Roger looked around at the commotion that had come of this apparently sudden disappearance, and then to the laboratory indicated by Marcus. Letting Marcus' voice fade into the background, he wasted little time examining the rather empty room. *"Why is his departure the cause for such a fuss?"* He wondered, but then let his mind run back over Marcus's words. He turned back towards the younger man, and raised a single index finger to interrupt.

"Wait a minute, wait a minute…his eyes? You mentioned this man's eyes. What about his eyes?" Roger Thascalos asked, recalling his assistant's fascination with the eyes of the hideous arachnids they had encountered at the Erebus household.

"They were extremely light sensitive," Marcus replied, having stopped his lengthy response to the Doctor's previous question. "They seemed to absorb and reflect any light source that he encountered, but the light seemed to cause him pain."

"Light sensitivity…light reflection," Doctor Thascalos said, ponderingly. He surveyed the large, empty laboratory, and noticed the discarded cloak. "Has that cloak been analyzed? Do you have any medical data on Lupo?" Taking a deep breath, he realized that he didn't want to add to the level of panic that was already present in the Experimental Sciences Department. The younger man seemed stymied by the Doctor's interest, and before he could formulate a reply, Doctor Thascalos spoke up once again. "I wonder if this could be related to the events I witnessed at the Erebus residence."

Looking at the one security monitor that was still running, the Doctor was surprised to find that it was the Erebus household that the surveillance camera was fixed upon.

"Erebus?" the younger man repeated.

"Yes?" Roger Thascalos replied abruptly and impatiently; the image of the property on the screen causing him to once again visualize, with horrifying clarity, the image of poor Jack

Erebus being surrounded and absorbed by the mass of the eight-legged arachnids. "What about it?" He asked curiously, the image in his mind fading to reveal the real-time image of an athletic blonde approaching the house that he had cordoned off with the barricade. He watched in dismay as she seemed to be drawn towards the glowing light emanating from a hole in the wall, and panic arose within him, as she quickly moved to enter the house.

"Erebus…" Marcus Peirama seemed fixed on the name, but finally continued his thought process. "Erebus is…was Lupo's last name."

A silence immediately followed, both professionals stared at one another in quizzical amazement and uncertainty of what to say or do next. The sight of the blonde, who was most likely Jack Erebus' wife, approaching the hole from which the spiders had swarmed was pushed aside by what Marcus had just revealed to him. The revelation that the man that Doctor Thascalos had encountered at the site of the unusual readings, and the mysterious scientist who had disappeared around the same time, both shared the same name was clearly more than a coincidence. *"But what does it all mean?"* the Doctor asked himself in his mind.

While the Doctor stood there looking perplexed, staring at the cloak that lay across the stool in front of the main computer terminal, Marcus stepped away to answer a ringing telephone. Moments later, he returned to Lupo's laboratory, and addressed Thascalos.

"Doctor Thascalos? There's a phone call for you, a Mr. Nidell?" Marcus reported swiftly.

"Eric..." Roger Thascalos muttered under his breath. Nodding, he stepped out of the room towards the phone that rested off of its receiver. "Hello? Eric? Eric, slow down...what, Wolf Spiders...what? Eric! Eric, what's wrong?!? ...Eric?"

CHAPTER 24

FAMILIAR FACES

QUANTUS ENTERPRISES:
LOBOS CHAMBER #314
12:42am, Sunday, November 25th, 2018

As Miles awoke upon yet another unfamiliar surface, the light above him shone brightly in his eyes as he tried to open them. He groaned and raised his hand towards it, then tried to shake his hand in a downwards gesture which had worked before, but to no effect. But then the light was suddenly switched off, and he hesitantly tried to open his eyes again. His gaze was met by pure and total darkness, and then a different light was suddenly switched on, and he cried out in frustration of being almost blinded again.

"Sorry, sorry!" he heard an unfamiliar voice taking responsibility for the sudden change in lighting. "I wasn't quite sure where the switch was and activated it accidentally before I could give you any warning."

The voice was completely unrecognizable and new to Miles, but he once again managed to open his eyes and slowly moved to sit up to see who was speaking to him. As his head lifted up off the hard metal surface, he winced and groaned again, almost falling back once more as he reached for the back of his neck.

"Owww, dammit, what the devil hit me?" he finally spoke, then his eyes widened at the thought that perhaps he was speaking to his assailant. "Or should I ask who?"

Administrator Thascalos was intelligent enough to recognize that reaction, and was quick to address it.

"Rest assured, my good sir, that I am not responsible for your assault, or for you being here." Peter took a slow deep sigh, and then continued. "In fact, I indirectly managed to prevent you from being potentially killed, or worse!"

Miles pushed to sit up again so that he could face the man with whom he was having this discussion. Observing the clean shaven gentleman wearing a white lab coat, he tried to figure out where he was, and why. His eyes gradually moved around the technological gizmos and screens that surrounded him, and then observed the slumped figure of a red haired lady on a chair, which swiftly brought his attention back to the man by the light switch.

"How long have I been unconscious?" Miles asked, wincing. His neck throbbed painfully, impairing his ability to think clearly, so it took him a moment to ask the more important questions that had to be asked. "Wait, who are you? And who is she?" he gestured to the unconscious female in the easy chair.

"My name is Peter Thascalos, I am the Administrator of the Science & Technology Department, here at Quantus Enterprises." Peter proudly started the introductions, gesturing to the newest addition to the Quantus staff. "This lovely Irish lass..."

"Hang on…" Miles interrupted abruptly, wincing as the conversation aggravated the pounding in his head, and his neck continued to throb. "Quantus? We're in the Quantus Enterprises building?" The name rang an alarming bell for him.

"Yes, and it seems that you have heard of it." Peter deduced, based on the stranger's reactions. "As I was saying, the young lady here is my short-term assistant, the newest member in my department, Ms. Anita O'Dell. And, may I ask who you are, sir?"

"My name is Miles, Miles Militis." Miles tried to calm himself, since Dr. Thascalos seemed disinclined to harm him. "From your lab coat, I wondered at first if you were part of the Scientific Unity Complex." Miles slowly swung his legs around to the floor and carefully climbed off of the hard medical table. Glancing back at it curiously, he returned his gaze to Dr. Thascalos. "I still don't know what exactly has been going on here."

"Well, I'm afraid that I probably don't have *all* of the answers for you," Peter replied. "I *do* know that I have seen video surveillance footage of you, shortly after you first arrived here in Amgine City. But who you are, why you are here, and why you were laying on that surgical table are all questions that I do not have answers for, as of yet."

Anita O'Dell moaned her face contorting as she stiffly moved to sit upright in the chair. Slowly opening her eyes, she took in the unfamiliar space of Grylos' domain. She breathed a sigh of relief when she discovered the Administrator standing there looking at her, but then she saw Miles standing near a medical table and was once again perplexed.

"Umm, good morning," she spoke, taking a wild guess as to

the time of day. "I think…" Clearing her throat, she tried again, "Administrator? Could you tell me what is going on?"

Poor Peter Thascalos was unable to find the time to find answers for himself, and here these two others were trying to get similar answers from him. He frowned at Anita, and then at Miles, then he returned his attention towards her.

"As I was just explaining to Miles here," Peter began, but then paused. "Oh, by the way, this is our mysterious visitor to the city, a Mr. Miles Militis. The man who was somehow transported to our dimension, by a means somehow related to Project Weltschmerz." He waited until they silently acknowledged one another with a nod before continuing. "I came to this section of the Quantus Enterprises building to talk to Grylos, one of our more unique scientists. It seems that I came at an inopportune moment for him, as I found you shackled and hanging from the wall, and Miles here was laid unconscious on that table. It is unclear what Grylos' true intentions were but, before either of you awoke, he collapsed and…" Biting his bottom lip, he wasn't sure if he could put it into words, he still couldn't believe it himself; even after seeing it with his own eyes. "He just disappeared, faded into nothingness. I'm still trying to work out why or how that could've happened, and have lost track of the whereabouts of his visually impaired assistant completely."

"Visually impaired…ohhh, so now it makes more sense," Miles interrupted. "At least, a little bit more sense." Feeling the eyes of both his companions fixed upon him, he cleared his throat and tried to explain. "Well, that's actually the last thing that I remember. I was helping this blind woman across the street, I'd accidentally turned a corner and walked right into her, nearly knocking her off of her feet, so I felt it was the least that I could do. She seemed to be rather unsteady on her feet, even after I escorted her to the other side of the street, so I continued to help her along her way." The throbbing in Miles' neck was starting to intensify, causing him to wince again. "We'd managed to get past this one building, there was a dark alley and…then I felt something hit me." Reaching for the back of his neck, near the base of his skull, "The next thing I knew, I was waking up to a blinding light, and not for the first time since arriving here, mind you, and meeting the Administrator."

Peter considered the story that he had just heard carefully and nodded slowly.

"It would appear that you were very carefully baited by Grylos and his assistant," the Administrator concluded. "I'm not entirely certain why he was so interested in you that he would go to such extreme lengths; though I am also curious about your presence here, as Ms. O'Dell will attest to."

Anita wasn't giving her full attention to what Peter was saying, her mind working through the story that Miles just described, and trying to recall her own last memory before waking up in this strange room.

A hush washed over all three occupants of Grylos' domain, none of them feeling certain about what to say or do next.

CENTRUS LABORATORIES:
RESEARCH LAB #2
1:42pm, Sunday, October 26th, 2014

Doctor Thascalos returned to his lab to find his apprentice Eric in a state of panic.

"Eric, what's going on? What's wrong?" Roger addressed his unusually emotional subordinate.

"I was right...about everything," Eric said, in an almost trance-like monotone voice. "The spiders we'd encountered at the Erebus residence, I originally deduced, were Wolf Spiders; based on their preference for the dark, and their ability to reflect the light in their eyes. But, then I..."

"Lupo apparently had a similar trait," The Doctor interrupted, reporting what he had been told during his visit to the Experimental Sciences department. "The scientist that disappeared, rather inexplicably, apparently had a strong sensitivity to light, and what's more, his last name...was Erebus!"

Eric Nidell was irritated by the interruption, but hearing the name Erebus again caused him to quickly review what the Doctor had just told him.

"That's...beyond strange." Eric said, unable to find better words to describe what he was feeling.

"It gets worse," the Doctor warned him. "While I was in Lupo's laboratory, I saw a security surveillance monitor that recorded a blonde haired woman approaching the glowing hole in the wall and then rushing into the house!"

Eric's eyes gave a completely stunned look; better than Roger had seen anyone do before. Roger shook his head in disbelief of all that was happening.

"There's something we're missing from all of this," Thascalos deduced. "Something we are both overlooking."

"I recommend that we go back there and see if we can save her!" Eric suggested. While not one of Eric's most well-considered suggestions, The Doctor did not hesitate to agree, and the two men hurried towards the exit.

☉☉☉

QUANTUS ENTERPRISES:
LOBOS CHAMBER #314
1:03am, Sunday, November 25th, 2018

The hush in Grylos' domain was becoming eerie and unbearable for all 3 occupants, until finally one spoke up.

"I think I should retrace my steps," Miles Militis was the first to speak. "Maybe find some clue in that alley where I was attacked."

"If you are feeling up to the walk, and don't mind some company," Administrator Thascalos responded to the suggestion. "I believe that Ms. O'Dell could use some fresh air…" He looked around the room where quite a few unusual events occurred in such a short time, then coughed abruptly. "I know I could!"

Miles looked at the other 2 in the room, and did not hesitate to agree with the offer to accompany him.

"You know this facility better than I do," Miles logically concluded. "So why don't you lead the way?" He moved and gestured towards Anita, offering his hand for hers to help her to her feet. The three of them left the building together. Miles struggled to catch his bearings as he looked around. "I'm looking for Giovanni's Pizza Palace, that's the last place that I remember being before encountering the blonde whom you say was assisting this…Grylos, was it?."

"Ah yes, it's this way!" The Administrator nodded and pointed to the east. The trio gradually advanced in the direction indicated, determined to work together to find answers.

☉☉☉

SCIENTIFIC UNITY COMPLEX: SECURITY CHAMBER K-1
1:14am, Sunday, November 25th, 2018

"Professor, I've found him!" Security Officer Murdoch announced, as the security tracers picked up the signal from Miles' tablet.

"Excellent, excellent...wait..." Olim Archaios' pleased expression washed away swiftly as some unusual readings began registering. "What the hell? It isn't time for that yet!" He slammed his aged fist against the desk in frustration before turning away with a look of disbelief. "What will they think?" He asked himself aloud, staring at a partly obscured panel in the wall.

☉☉☉

AMGINE CITY: DOWNTOWN
1:20am, Sunday, November 25th, 2018

The area began looking a bit more familiar to Miles, who was helping the semi-limp form of Ms. O'Dell walk along the street. Anita started to groan and whimper, the Administrator turned to check on her and realized that something was amiss.

"Miles, you will have to go on without us," Peter Thascalos suggested. "Anita is too weak to continue. If you stay along this road here, you'll be back at Giovanni's in a little under three minutes."

"Thank you," Miles responded with utmost respect for the professional who clearly had his best intentions at heart. The three split up, and just as Miles was approaching Giovanni's, he witnessed all of the lights inside and outside the restaurant, followed by the street lights and surrounding buildings, even the Quantus Glider in the sky...every light source within a clearly visible radius had suddenly blinked out, and the city succumbed to total, sudden, and enigmatic darkness.

"Earth Hour..." Miles muttered to himself quietly, observing the odd happenings around him, but something wasn't right. *"This...this is TOO dark!"* he pondered quietly. His eyes were drawn towards something that didn't quite fit in with all of this pitch blackness. Waiting for the mysterious object to come into focus, he muttered to himself openly, "It's been some 15 years since I've seen a blackout like this."

"14 years, actually, to be more accurate," stated a voice in the darkness. Miles turned around to find the source of the voice, what he found caused his eyes to widen in shock and disbelief.

"Hello Miles, my old friend, it's good to see you." When the man stepped out of the shadows, and into the gradually increasing lone source of light, from an object that was fast approaching their location, Miles recognized him at once.

"Jack?" Miles gasped, "What the hell are you doing here?"

"I think," Jack Erebus started, taking a step closer, "That is precisely the question that I ought to be asking you, Miles."

CHAPTER 25

CONVERGENCE

Miles stood dumbfounded, ironically much like a deer in the headlights, as the approaching light source turned out to be the headlights of Velvet's car. As the vehicle pulled up between the two men, Miles went from dumbfounded by the encounter with his best friend's husband to being quite surprised that it was Velvet pulling up in her vehicle in front of him. The passenger side door flew open.

"Miles! Get in, quick!" Velvet said, clearly panicked as she cried out from the driver's seat. Miles was in no real position to hesitate, and swiftly climbed into the vehicle; barely having time to close the door before she sped off towards Malum City.

"I don't know what all this is about," Velvet lamented, trying to keep calm. "Between your tablet being tracked, and now this loss of power in the main city…and whoever the hell that was who was facing off with you; but we need to talk to Josef."

"That was, um…" Miles could hardly believe it, let alone bring himself to mention his friend's name. "So these lights aren't all out to appease the mass majority, and the MOTH Squad, for

Earth Hour?" he asked, switching the subject to what he hoped was a less confusing one.

"Earth Hour isn't until tomorrow night, Miles!" Velvet growled, speeding towards the entrance of Depravus Tower. Not even bothering to find a spot in the underground parking lot, she shut the vehicle down hastily and pressed the button to open both front doors. "We need Josef's help and resources to figure out what is going on, and why!"

🕐🕑🕒

THE EREBUS RESIDENCE
1:42pm, Sunday, October 26th, 2014

As one might've predicted, Doctor Roger Thascalos and Eric Nidell his dedicated Asian apprentice were too late to do anything about Angelique Lambros-Erebus' fate.

This time, Eric had brought some more sophisticated equipment with him. Despite the warnings of his superior, he anxiously approached the Erebus house, oblivious to the dark energy cloud that had formed, and was growing overhead.

"Eric...ER–IC!!! Come back!" Roger called but Eric had already entered the home of Jack and Angelique Lambros-Erebus through the side door, which was, for some strange reason, ajar.

Against his better judgment, Doctor Thascalos followed his assistant, hoping to avoid providing another victim to the swarm of spiders which were bound to make a return appearance at any moment.

"Eric, wait..." he called again, seeing the back end of Eric making his way towards the basement, using a remote tracker to determine where Angelique had gone. "The sky, Eric, the sky... it's going dark again. It's too dangerous to stay here. Eric, are you listening to me?"

The Doctor was becoming more frustrated with his inability to establish a dialogue with his fellow scientist. Before Doctor Thascalos could follow, Eric was entering the spare bedroom next to the wine cellar and the door slammed shut between them and locked. Thascalos, fearing his partner was being trapped by some unknown force, cried "*Eric! No!*"

Hearing a very unusual groan from the room that echoed throughout the house, Thascalos realized he was possibly about to face something that he could not handle, and turned to race back up the stairs; sprinting outside and back to the perimeter fencing, hoping it was still the safest place to observe what was going on.

Reaching the car outside the barricade, Thascalos sat panting for a moment as he watched the dark patch continue to spread across the horizon, his eyes widening in horror of what it could possibly mean. Hearing some unusual bleeps and clicks from inside the vehicle, the doctor turned to discover that Eric had left a machine inside the vehicle for short-range communication. Eric was only able to send out a few random, but potentially vital words before being overcome by the unseen forces that claimed the Erebus household.

"Nocturnal phenomenon, Wolf Spider, Dream Spider... Quantubus Effect," Doctor Thascalos read aloud the message left behind by his doomed subordinate. Climbing into the car and closing the door behind him, he quickly put the vehicle into "Drive" and sped out of the neighbourhood, hoping to return to where there was still some blue sky. "I will figure this out, Eric;

I swear your last words will not be in vain." He spoke aloud, providing himself with a sense that Eric was still with him.

☉☉☉

MALUM CITY:
DEPRAVUS TOWER
2:03am, Sunday November 25th, 2018

Velvet burst through the entrance to the main hall of Depravus Tower, startling both Tim and Josef, as Miles followed in her wake.

"Mr. Militis, welcome back to Depravus Tower." Josef Aros greeted his returning guest. "It would appear that your presence here in Amgine City, or indeed in this realm, has stirred up quite the temporal hornet's nest."

"'Temporal hornet's nest'," Miles repeated, "Yes, I suppose it has! Though, the last thing that I ever wanted to do, ever since first waking up inside the Scientific Unity Complex, is cause trouble. Do you have any thoughts on how to handle the situation, or any details that you can share with me, so that I may be able to help develop some ideas?"

Josef silently directed Velvet and Tim to sit down, then gestured politely for Miles to do the same. "Tim, why don't you fill our guest in on what we know about this sudden dark phenomenon?" the elder leader of the poorly named "Bullet Squad" suggested to his young associate.

"Yes sir, Josef," he said, then turned his attention towards their guest. "Hello again, Miles, good to see you, and I am so glad to see that you do not appear to have been harmed during the goings on of late; and thankfully relieved that you were also not the cause." This remark is met with a quizzical look by Miles, wanting to obviously hear more about the "goings on". The excited, or perhaps nervous, young man continued his report. "Well, this most recent occurrence, this sudden blackout, has caught much of Amgine City off guard. Fortunately, our team has discovered some unusual anomalies, which actually were by design. You see, my team-mates and I are technically responsible for the blackout."

"*What?*" Miles exclaimed, interrupting the report. "What possible justification could you have for sapping the metropolis of Amgine City of its power sources?"

"Please, let me continue, Miles," Tim suggested. "A number of us were determined to discover how the MOTH Squad were able to learn who was planning to subvert their initiatives, and where to find the rebels. What we did *not* expect to find, was something that our security trackers picked up after the power went down." He pulled down a screen from its ceiling suspension, and dimmed the surrounding illumination, which was ironic considering the screen was depicting the darkness that enveloped Amgine City. But then a luminous sight appeared on the screen, and Tim halted the video. "As you can see, Quantus Enterprises, there" he pointed to one of the 2 areas of light on the screen, then drew attention to the other. "And the Scientific Unity Complex there, are clearly not connected to the main power source that keeps the city running! Our in-depth scanners have actually detected some kind of anomalous underground power source that is connected to both." Turning off the video screen, Velvet assisted by turning the portable generator back on; which returned the lighting level in the room back to normal. "The most daunting and damning thing of all is, we cannot identify what kind of energy is being used from that power source, it's like nothing we've ever seen, encountered, or registered before."

Miles reflected back upon his most recent visit to the Complex, wondering if perhaps Professor Olim Archaios was pre-occupied by something that he was labouring to keep secret. Miles stared blankly for a few moments, weighing this potential, and then finally shook his head clear.

"All right, we know there's something strange going on at the Complex," Miles spoke up, trying to sound resolute. "What are we going to do about it?"

Suddenly, all eyes were on Miles, and that gave him a severe case of butterflies in the stomach. Looking sheepishly at the 3 other people in the room, he nervously looked behind his shoulder to see if perhaps they weren't actually staring at him, but there was nothing and nobody there.

"'*We* are not going to do as much as *you* are going to do, my young friend." Josef finally broke the awkward silence. "We want you to return to the Complex one more time, gain entry, and confront your contact on the inside for some answers that we desperately need. This power outage will not last long, so you will have to act fast."

Miles felt the pressure of time upon him once again, but the same thought recurred in his mind, and he finally arose from his seat and stared directly at Josef.

"I have one alteration to suggest for this game plan," he started, staring intently at Josef. "I would like you to accompany me, and meet the Professor yourself."

There was another unsteady hush that washed over the 4 of them, but finally Josef arose from his seat and nodded curtly, accepting the invitation; the two men silently agreeing to be investigators and ambassadors at the same time, as they turned towards the exit and left together.

CENTRUS LABORATORIES:
RESEARCH LAB #2
3:03pm, Sunday, October 26th, 2014

Doctor Roger Thascalos could not help but feel a deep sense of loss and sadness. Now being left to work out the rest of this odd series of events on his own, however, he quickly moved towards the main computer terminal to try and pick up the trail of research progress that Eric had left behind.

As Roger punched in the handful of references that Eric had provided, likely his final words, a pattern began to emerge. .

"Ohhh, Eric…" he muttered to an assumed spirit, or at least the lingering essence of his late apprentice. "If only you could've told me about some of this before…"

CHAPTER 26

THE THIRD WORLD

MALUM CITY:
DEPRAVUS TOWER
2:03am, Sunday, November 25th, 2018

Josef took the driver's seat of Velvet's unique vehicle, and Miles climbed into the passenger seat; the seatbelts automatically fastened them in before the vehicle sped towards the heart of Amgine City.

Being particularly vigilant, aiding the elder gentleman in these dark streets, Miles spotted a flaming torch being waved on a side street and nudged Josef to get his attention.

"Wait, over there," Miles called out urgently, causing Josef to slow down and turn onto the next side street that he could find to loop around. "Someone seems to be in dire need of assistance. I saw what looked like someone waving some kind of a flaming torch."

Turning to the right again, they found the side street with the lone flame lighting up the curb area. Miles was astonished to discover Administrator Thascalos of Quantus Enterprises was the torch bearer. Pulling alongside, Miles finally figured out how to open his window.

"Peter! What are you doing over here?" Miles asked. "Where's Anita?"

"Hello Miles," Peter leaned forward and eyed Josef, "And thank you, Sir, for coming back around to me." Dousing his torch and disposing of it carefully, he turned to Miles'. "Anita is fine. I helped her to find a safe haven. As it transpired, she lives near Giovanni's Pizza Palace, so that was ideal. I searched the streets to see if I could find anyone else about. I didn't want to be mistaken for a marauder, so I found this torch like branch and figured out a way to get it lit. Would you two gentlemen mind if I joined you? My legs and feet are killing me."

Josef considered the plea being made by the stranger, whom Miles evidently trusted, and activated a switch that extended the vehicle's length enough to incorporate more passengers. After opening the back door to allow the clean shaven man in the lab coat to enter the vehicle, they resumed their travels towards the Complex.

"It's good to see you again, Miles." The exhausted scientist said, "And a pleasure to meet you sir," he said to Josef. "My name is Peter Thascalos, and I'm the Administrator of the Science & Technology Division of Quantus Enterprises. Where are we heading?"

"I'm Josef Aros," Josef said, cautiously avoiding revealing his too much about himself as he responded to their new passenger. "We are en route to the Scientific Unity Complex; to investigate some unusual...reports that we have received of late." Josef hesitated to use the word "readings" while trying to hide his true identity from a scientist.

The vehicle had finally arrived at its destination. The brightly lit exterior of the Scientific Unity Complex allowed one to more accurately observe its odd shape and design. More and more, Miles had the impression that this was an important clue as to the origins of the Complex, its inhabitants, and perhaps…its power source.

As the most familiar of the three to the staff inside the Complex, Miles was the one to step forward and activate the communications panel.

"Welcome back Mr. Militis," the familiar voice of Olim Archaios could be heard through some slight crackling on the other side of the speaker. "We were not anticipating your visit at this time, and that in itself is unusual, as we've been tracking your movements since your last visit."

"That's because we were able to put a jamming signal on the tracker on his tablet before we came out here." Josef stepped forward and addressed the disembodied voice sternly. The implied accusation led to a pregnant silence before the speaker crackled once again.

"I see, and what is the purpose of your visit, if I may ask?" Archaios struggled to remain calm and professional, uncertain as to the origins of the man who spoke last.

"Professor Archaios," Miles started, "We are wanting to learn why your Complex is almost the only place around that still has power enough to illuminate a good portion the street from its own lighting source? May we be permitted entry?"

"Thank you, Mr. Militis," Archaios after another brief silence. "As a precaution, I feel I must warn you that I will be placing your companions under your responsibility. If they should take any aggressive action, we will consider you *all* hostile."

The door hummed and clicked before sliding open. Miles stepped in first and led the rest of them to where he assumed the Professor would be waiting for him, in his office. He was taken aback when a secret door panel slid open from out of nowhere, with the elderly Professor Archaios being escorted by two security officers.

"Welcome gentlemen," Olim Archaios addressed them as if he hadn't spoken to any of them just a few moments before. "You are just in time for the show."

The three men looked curiously at their host but followed him as he turned and led the way into Security Chamber K-1. One whole wall of the chamber was lined with various technical instruments and monitors, while the rest of the room, separated by a silvery border along some very different floor panelling, was clearly designed more for comfort and group discussions.

"Please gentlemen, have a seat, I promise you will not be disappointed by what I have to show you." The Professor was beaming brightly and moving rather sprightly for someone of such advanced years. "I can only hope that what I am about to show you will help answer any questions that you may have, and resolve any issues you may have encountered." There was something almost eerie about the gentleman's sudden bend towards the diplomatic approach. All three visitors found a seat and, as Miles had experienced with the first chair he'd sat upon in the Complex, each adjusted to the weight and comfort requirements of each individual.

The Professor gestured for the lights to be dimmed, but Administrator Thascalos interrupted him with a raised hand.

"Excuse me, Professor," Thascalos spoke. "But it seems that not all of us have been properly introduced to each other yet."

"Of course, of course, my apologies for putting your seemingly urgent business ahead of social niceties," The Professor apologized. "My name is Professor Olim Archaios, and I am one of the lead personnel here at the Complex." Both Peter Thascalos and Josef Aros introduced themselves in turn, resolving the diplomatic faux pas.

"Excellent, now without further ado," the Professor once again gestured for the lights to be turned down, and the planned holographic presentation began to run on the screen in front of and around them. The slim platinum line that bordered between the 2 sets of floor tiles was revealed to be a well-hidden invisible video wall that allowed for 360 degree visuals to be displayed. "This, my dear fellow citizens, is the Liberus realm." Professor Olim Archaios introduced, in his tutorial tone. "You will note that we have acquired a rare holo-video recording that will adjust to various viewpoints over time." He then promptly ceased his narration and let the show commence, allowing the footage to speak for itself.

The holographic display was meticulously detailed as what it represented was both daunting and hard to believe. Here, it showed the audience the environment of yet another, different but very real, version of the Earth that they each knew and recognized. The 3-D holograph camera drone that was used to acquire this footage moved down from the top of the CN Tower towards a small suburban neighbourhood, and was able to capture it from all sides, which allowed the presentation to envelop the spectators from all angles.

As it drifted along the neighbourhood, two things were immediately noticeable, and strange. Houses appeared to have no front doors, and there seemed to be a great abundance of clones walking the streets. Locations, vistas, and landmarks all appeared similar to that which each man could recognize and identify.

Upon arriving at the end of one street, the incredible demonstration halted. Professor Archaios stepped forward and directed their attention to one particular building.

"As you can see," Archaios started eagerly, "this alternate dimension also had its own version of our Quantus Enterprises." The sign on the marquee in front of the building read "LIBERUS FOUNDATION". Striding further along the illusion of the visual landscape, the Professor continued to narrate. "This dimension clearly seems to embrace cloning to a greater extent than the WE-DOO Triumvirate could have possibly even considered allowing us to do. This footage, and all of the recoverable documentation that was found with the holographic data crystal we've discovered, sadly, does not provide sufficient details as to how the cloning was achieved, nor whether it was also used in the advancement of medical science. However, as there seemed to be a great many clones walking around, one has to assume that this particular society did not take that path, in favour of allowing its citizens to clone themselves merely for amusement or perhaps to simply sustain a consistent population."

Ceasing his narrative, the Professor sat down and the demonstration resumed. This section of the footage depicted a rather sophisticated looking laboratory. The three-dimensional nature of the presentation had diminished however, seeming more like someone was recording using an advanced version of a handheld video camera. As the camera drew nearer to a man in a white lab coat, the man turned sharply with a look of surprise on his face. The man's face exhibited a few scars and a black patch over his left eye. The playback was frozen once more as Archaios faced his companions again, noting the look of shock on Administrator Thascalos' face.

"Yes, Peter," Archaios confirmed. "As you can see, this depiction of an alternate, but parallel, Earth had its own professional named Thascalos, a Superintendent Anthony Thascalos, to be more specific. There's not much in the way of detail regarding his injuries, but I really halted here to draw more direct attention towards the screen in the background." Adjusting a dial on the remote control device in his hand, Archaios zoomed in on the computer monitor beyond Superintendent Thascalos' left shoulder. At first, it appeared that Archaios was focusing on the date, which clearly read "February 2 2020", but then he revealed his true target. The term "**QUANTUBUS EFFECT**" was suddenly quite clearly visible on the screen, in a bright and bold shade of red. This revelation caused a few disturbed murmurs from the on-lookers. The display blinking off before the lights went back up didn't help calm them either.

"Apologies, gentlemen, there is more to see, but we have had an issue with our display module." Archaios maintained his diplomatic composure to try and keep order and civility among his guests. "Please stand by…"

CHAPTER 27

CASCADING THEORY

CENTRUS LABORATORIES:
RESEARCH LAB #2
3:58pm, Sunday, October 26th, 2014

Doctor Roger Thascalos was deeply engrossed in his research at Centrus Laboratories; so focused on finding the answers that his assistant Eric died to help him discover, that he hadn't realized that the phone had been ringing.

"*Of course,*" he muttered and then "Why didn't I see that? Eric, you really were a genius!" Perhaps becoming a bit unhinged by the sudden and unfortunate loss of his assistant, he continued to address the unseen presence that he sensed was there in the room with him. "Quantubus, nocturnal phenomenon…one only needed to look into similar phenomenon to realize what had gone wrong!"

"Incubus, Succubus, Quantubus!!!" Doctor Thascalos proclaimed triumphantly. "That explains why those nasty arachnids at the Erebus household were no ordinary spiders, not even your typical Wolf Spider, but *Dream Spiders*; a mutated form of Wolf Spider that thrived on the darkness, and on the energy of gravitational waves to create the Quantubus Effect!"

Suddenly, Doctor Roger Thascalos froze in place; captured in the act of leaning over the computer console in a pose similar to the one Superintendent Anthony Thascalos was seen in during the Liberus Realm Holo-Recording.

"So you see, my dear fellows," Professor Archaios started up his narrative efforts again, gesturing to the frozen image of Doctor Thascalos. "Not only is the Centrus realm further behind in time and technology, but they are also, somewhat inexplicably, further behind in other ways as well. And yet, this footage we have just witnessed indicates that there were those in that realm who had the intelligence, skills, and resources to effect change and find the answers to some of the world's most pressing issues." Almost clicking off the footage again, he quickly called out "*lights?*" and the room was illuminated moments before the screens went dark.

"Now," He addressed his guests once again, "you gentlemen wanted to know more about how this Complex, and indeed the Quantus Enterprises building, are able to still have power when the rest of Amgine City lies in darkness." He paused, waiting for their reactions. He watched as they nodded their heads in unison, seemingly wanting to speak up but waiting instead for their host to continue. "Well, that is the most incredible part of this explanation that I have provided, though I don't have the most complete answer to that part as of yet. It seems the "Quantubus Effect" has occurred at least once in each of the 3 realities and also had some relation to Albert Einstein's Theory on Gravitational Waves." Professor Archaios was keen to continue his solo description of the findings made using the resources of the Complex, but he observed Administrator Thascalos' hand raised in the air. "Peter? Did you have something to add?"

"Yes, Professor," Peter Thascalos arose from his seat and addressed his host. "There is more to this mystery than even you are aware of. I've done plenty of research on technology, and have also done studies of unusual phenomenon that have occurred, particularly those witnessed or experienced by only a limited portion of the population. When Mr. Militis was transported to this realm, I noted some unusual, but oddly familiar readings on one of our lesser-used tracking computers, and investigated. I discovered a hidden, likely "presumed lost/discarded" file called "Project Weltschmerz". For those of you unaware of the term, Weltschmerz is a German term describing the mental depression or apathy caused by a comparison of the actual state of the world with an ideal state. So I have solid proof that there's much more going on here than just some random occurrences involving Dream Spiders and nocturnal phenomenon."

"Indeed there is!" a young voice announced proudly from down the hall. Moments later, Tim was seen escorting a prisoner in handcuffs…it was Jack Erebus!

"What the…Tim, what the hell is going on?" Miles was awe-struck to see his best friend's husband being manhandled and led around like a common criminal. What confused Miles even more was the fact that Jack seemed to have difficulty meeting his gaze.

"It's quite simple," Tim replied, "Velvet told me of the mystical appearance of a stranger when she picked you up; indicating that there was something just not quite right about him. I sent Josef's surveillance drone out to see if I could pick up the trail of what seemed to rub Velvet's "Spidey Sense" the wrong way." Shoving the prisoner deeper into the room, Archaios' henchman, Security Officer Murdoch, stepped forward, just in case Jack tried to escape while Tim was busy telling his story. "So, while you three took off to investigate things, we took my vehicle from the underground garage to see whether we could follow the drone and see what this fellow might be up to. Lo and behold, he was working his way into a sealed chamber inside the Quantus Enterprises building! Room 314, I believe was the number."

"Did you say Room 314?" Administrator Thascalos queried sharply, "That's Grylos' domain, where I found Miles and Anita being held!" Thascalos's eyes narrowed at the younger man in chains. "Do we know why he was trying to get into that particular room?"

"Oh, he let a few things slip when we apprehended him." Tim answered for his quiet captive. "But maybe we can hear him speak up for himself? I believe he has quite a tale to tell us all."

All eyes that were on Jack, Miles' was likely the pair of eyes that showed the most mixed emotions, seeing an old friend, but hearing so much about what that friend might've done.

"Fine, fine," Jack felt too much pressure not to speak up, and half-hoped that it might help his cause somehow to come clean. "For those of you who do not know, my name is Jack Erebus. What none of you know about me is that I come from the parallel dimension that is generally known as the Liberus Realm. I was in the midst of exploiting the technological resources of the Liberus Foundation building for my own gains. I realized that there had to be some better way to live than in a world of clones, despite having so many freedoms, that a citizen is expected to want for nothing. I enlisted the aid of a German scientist who was able to see things from my perspective, and together we tried to see what could be done about utilizing the cloning technology, and enhancing it to work on a temporal plane. The next thing I knew, some kind of spatial vortex opened, and I had been transported to a world quite dissimilar to my own, but clearly still Earth. It didn't take me long to realize though, that I'd gone from one extreme to the other. So many restrictions, so much death, the air was practically *poison* there was so much pollution; I'd also left behind the woman I loved in that reality, or so I thought."

Jack forced himself to pause, as his throat was getting very dry. He gestured to Tim to help him take a sip of ice water from the tray of glasses that sat on a table nearby. Being careful with his actions, so as not to arouse suspicion or concern, he took in a few refreshing gulps and then waved it away.

"Ah, thank you, Tim was it?" Jack eyed the younger man who nodded in acknowledgement. "Right, Tim, good…at any rate, I arrived at a version of my own home that was clearly in need of repairs, and approached the house to find that my own wife Angelique was there, in that very different reality, but it was the same Angelique! I even tested her, but made it appear to be a test for my own memory's sake. I'm not quite sure if there was another Jack Erebus running around who just happened to meet and marry the same girl, or if somehow she got sucked into the same vortex as I did." Taking another quick pause, he cleared his throat, "Anyways, to make a long story short…"

"Too late," both Josef Aros and Olim Archaios spoke in unison, and then smiled briefly at each other, before returning their attention to the others.

"This could help explain everything," Administrator Thascalos proclaimed, interrupting Jack's story further. "We know that there was a mysterious scientific figure present, both here and in the Centrus Realm, and we know that at least one of them also had the last name Erebus…"

"A side effect of the Cascading Convergence Phenomenon!"

Professor Olim Archaios spoke up and all eyes were immediately on him. He gestured to Josef and Miles, "Come with me. There's something I think you will want to see." the Professor addressed the youngest man in the room, "Tim, I feel you can be trusted to take charge of things here. If you need any assistance, Security Officer Murdoch there will be at your disposal."

"Follow me, gentlemen," Olim directed, "It is time for you to learn the answer to one of your most pressing questions." The Professor led his 2 invited guests through a different door that led to a downward staircase.

CHAPTER 28

THE DAY THE EARTH MOVED

Professor Olim Archaios led the way down the stairs; an intense thrumming noise could be heard from all around them as they neared the next solid platform. Archaios stepped aside and allowed his invited guests to enter, what a second door indicated was, the Dynami Cubiculum.

Neither Miles nor Josef were 100% certain what they were looking at, nor could they sense its nature from the ambient throbbing that surrounded them. However, the strangest part of this particular secret chamber was that the ground was covered with natural grass. Miles was the first to notice, and quickly nudged Josef to call his attention to it too. . Both men were caught staring as the Professor entered.

"*This*, my new friends," Olim started, once again brimming with enthusiasm, "*this* is where we get our power from. What we are standing on right now, is the source of that power; it is what remains of the Liberus Realm."

"*What?*" Miles shouted in shock, almost jumping back, as if not stepping upon the last remaining vestige of Nature from that realm would somehow help to preserve it.

"We here at the Complex have no idea how it came to be that our Earth would encapsulate and absorb a part of another." Archaios said, attempting to explain. "The Scientific Unity Complex didn't exist until this transition was discovered; which is why, as you may have noticed, the building is so oddly designed compared to the others in the downtown region of Amgine City."

Miles and Josef exchanged glances, then looked back down at the grass beneath their feet, and then up at the Professor.

"How could this have happened?" Josef was the first to speak, though Miles was wondering the same thing.

"I doubt that's a question that even Jack Erebus could answer," Professor Archaios shrugged, and then gestured towards the door. "Perhaps we should head back up and ask him?"

The three men left the heart of the Scientific Unity Complex, to return to the presentation room, where the others were still waiting. All three of the returning men focused their attentions toward Jack.

"Care to shed any more light on how you came to be in the Centrus Realm, Mr. Erebus?" Olim Archaios insisted on taking the lead in the investigation. Administrator Thascalos found the elderly gentleman's choice of words ironic, considering what they'd learned about the spiders at the Erebus household.

"Alright, I'll admit there is more," Jack started, his eyes meeting the gaze of several of the others in turn. "But what you must all understand is, I was not to know what would come of the experiment that the German scientist and I had run! There was some kind of spatial interference; some other force that was working both with us and against us at the same time. I never did learn what had come of him, or what that other source of power was."

"Gravity waves…" Peter Thascalos muttered aloud. "That spatial interference, the vortex portal that transported you…it must've also cloned you!" The Administrator was getting rather excited and piecing it all together. "The cloning factor in the equipment you were using must've worked to split you in 2 at the exact same moment as the serendipitous space/time transference occurred!"

All of the others stared blankly, with a hint of amazement at the middle-aged professional's conclusions. It *sounded* like things were making sense and coming together, but there was still something missing.

"The most puzzling thing of all, one thing I truly cannot explain," Jack uttered, unintentionally interrupting the Administrator's efforts to piece together the information being shared, "Is the abundant presence of those rather uncommon spiders in the foundation of my house! I can't figure out how they got there or why there were so many."

"The Dream Spiders," Administrator Thascalos concluded, "that must've been the Dream Spiders that my alternate doppelganger referred to during that brief recording we all witnessed earlier."

"Wolf Spiders, Dream Spiders, Cloning technology…time travel," Miles tried piecing it all together openly. "Quantubus… wait!" He turned sharply towards Professor Archaios. "That other Thascalos, Roger, was it? He mentioned Incubus and Succubus. Those are nocturnal phenomenon and, from what I know of them, somewhat mythological. But what if Quantubus and the

"Quantubus Effect" explains the Dream Spiders? Not as sexual a phenomenon as the other 2, Quantubus might have more to do with messing with time, space, and/or gravity waves?"

All eyes were on Miles as he then focused his attention on his best friend's husband while finally working through his own experiences and observations to help pull the facts together into one grand workable theory.

"Jack, you were not only sucked through to my home realm, you were also cloned, and splintered by this Cascade Convergence Phenomenon that Professor Archaios made reference to. Some as yet unknown force managed to manipulate the presence of the Liberus Realm's planet Earth, in order to utilize the gravitational waves that surrounded it. The timing was quite possibly completely coincidental, as it happened at the same time as you ran your experiment, causing the entire planet to be pulled through a similar rift in space/time; which explains why Liberus' Earth is now here in the Quantus Realm."

"Very impressive, Mr. Militis," Peter Thascalos interrupted, as Miles appeared to be running out of steam. "That all does tend to coincide with the file that I discovered hidden in the archives at the Quantus Enterprises building. Grylos was a splintered part of Jack Erebus' clone, which allowed him to maintain the knowledge of the Liberus experiment, and observe the end results. Perhaps a little too closely, considering his cybernetic limbs, glowing eyes, and the visual impairment of his blonde assistant."

"Ahhh yes, his blind assistant," Miles spoke up again, his eyes wide in shock as he exchanged glances with Jack. "Oh my goodness, that must've been Angelique's clone! *No wonder* she seemed so familiar to me!" Miles suddenly wondered if any of this had anything to do with those strange cascading ripples of colour and light that he'd observed since arriving in, what was obviously being referred to as, the Quantus Realm. He opted to keep that thought quiet as he looked around and tried to figure out what they all should do next.

Josef stepped forward, gazing at Tim and his still bound captive, and then over at Peter Thascalos.

"If I may make a recommendation on what to do next," the 120 plus year old African American gentleman captured the attention of everyone else in the room. "I think Mr. Erebus here should be let go, as his intentions were perhaps misguided, but not altogether malevolent. Mr. Thascalos there should return to the Quantus Enterprises building to see what else he can learn, now that more light has been shed upon some obscure fragments of established facts and observations. Tim, I think you can head back to Depravus Tower and return the city's power supply to normal." The twinkle in his eyes was ever-present now, being able to speak so freely; and so far away from the protection of his own domain. He turned his attention towards his fellow elder, Olim Archaios, "Would that be an acceptable set of suggestions, Professor Archaios?"

Olim Archaios nodded slowly. He'd seen a new side of the leader of the so-called "Bullet Squad", and nodded slowly.

"Yes, Mr. Aros," Professor Archaios replied. "And I believe that I have another set of plans to put into motion, something unique, special, and historic for many of us to partake in, once power and order are restored."

CHAPTER 29

THE UNFORGIVEN

With a great many truths now revealed, mysteries unravelled, hostilities ceased, and understandings reached, it was time for the CAN-DO Triumvirate, and even the WE-DOO Government, to finally acknowledge the deeds and efforts of great men, unsung heroes of the community, like Professor Olim Archaios and Josef Aros, along with his band of alleged "misfits".

Professor Archaios, utilizing his governing influences, arranged to put together this unique gathering of citizens of Amgine City for the most historic event to take place in the past 18 years. Together with a now-liberated Jack Erebus, and Miles Militis, Olim joined the 120+ year old Josef Aros on a grand stage set up just outside the fenced off border of Malum City. Each took turns proudly shaking hands with the formerly infamous leader of the rebellious faction that had led a very covert existence in the exiled shadows outside of Amgine City.

As an official honoured representative of one of the main governing bodies of the city, Professor Archaios was given the option to either be presented with a token of gratitude by a WE-DOO government representative, or to introduce Josef for the same honour. Being the selfless individual that he was known to be, and knowing that the site of the gathering was of particular significance to Josef Aros, he chose to speak first, and ascended to the podium outside of the barbed wire fence, which separated Amgine City from Malum City, on Ninth Street. The Professor smiled at the attending members of the community, and spoke with a sense of relief in his voice.

"I am proud to have lived long enough to see this day." Archaios began. "A day when this fence would no longer be needed and our fine metropolis would be whole once more." Applause and cheers roared from the crowd, but gradually grew silent, and the speaker continued. "While it is true, that I have voluntarily been granted the singular honour and privilege to recognize a fellow elder, for his abundant efforts to help keep, what may have falsely been believed to be the "criminal element" in check, this day would not be possible, were it not for the efforts of another fine gentleman. This man came to our City as an unknown stranger; our medical diagnostic systems could not identify him, nor could our most advanced computers explain how he came to be here. I was the first person to communicate with this young fellow, and somehow I knew that he would make a profound difference to the purposeful efforts of the Scientific Unity Complex. Little did I know, however, just how grand an impact he would truly end up making for our entire city! It seems appropriate for me to introduce you all to this…saviour, for lack of a better word. After all, he is a man who knows our honoured guest better than I do." The Professor paused with a smile; a few laughs followed from the crowd. "So, it is my pleasure to introduce to you, the newest citizen to arrive and be welcomed to Amgine City, Mr. Miles Militis!"

Miles stepped forward and stood beside Professor Archaios at the podium, smiling and waving to the cheering attendees; shaking hands with the Professor in appreciation as holograph recordings and traditional style pictures were taken from various angles. He guided the elderly gentleman to his seat next to the podium, before stepping up to the microphone himself.

"Thank you, Professor Archaios," Miles started. "When I first arrived in this realm, I had no idea where I was or why or what I would experience. Nor did I know what I would see when I explored this city, and encountered its inhabitants. I am very grateful to Olim Archaios for having taken the time and effort to get acquainted with me, to give me a chance, and to help me learn how to adapt to my new surroundings. Of course, a reflection upon my short time in this community would not be complete without giving due and proper credit to the man who I am proud to help honour here today. This man has wisdom beyond his 120 years, a great deal of patience, and undeniable integrity. I am pleased to call him my friend, and to have him come up to say a few words as we honour him and all that he has done to keep Malum City from becoming the symbol of shame that it was purported to be. Ladies and gentlemen, I proudly introduce to you a man who, has made a worthy enough contribution to society to be granted clearance, by the CAN-DO Triumverate, for living past the Century Life Mandate, the overseer of the, now former, Malum City...Mr. Josef Aros!"

Many in attendance cheered and applauded with abundant enthusiasm as Aros ascended the steps towards the podium. It was a moment of celebration, rejoicing and open expressions of appreciation. Unfortunately, the festivities were abruptly halted almost before they could really begin. Josef Aros's forward motion was halted, as his back arched before slumping forward, as he collapsed into the luckily positioned arms of Miles and the Professor. The 122 year old gentleman was gently lowered to the ground at their feet, the lively twinkle having dimmed one last time.

A new wave of panic and uncertainty quickly spread through the crowd. The mob of people encircling the celebrated gentleman murmured in not-so-silent hushes. Silent, unspoken concerns about whether Malum City was the violence haven that it was believed to be after all were pondered by many in attendance. The Professor checked for any signs of life, and for any indications of the cause of Josef's death.

In the end, what was initially believed to be the result of shock, or overwhelming emotion, turned out to be a fatal and silent gunshot, through the back, and into Josef's aged heart.

Once the cause of death was determined, it didn't take long to find the man who had pulled the trigger; a renegade member of the MOTH Squad! The other squad members in attendance ascended the interior of the building adjacent to Depravus Tower, and apprehended the assassin. They led him to a launch pad on the roof and swiftly moved to load him into a helicopter, to be taken to a prison facility. The condemned man shook himself free of the grips of his former colleagues, and glared down at the citizens below, focusing his attention upon the deceased old man and his companions. The man showed no signs of pity or shame, as he spat indignantly on the roof ledge.

"He was the leader of the Bullet Squad," he muttered, "And a constant thorn in our professional sides, I did you boys a favour... and gave him a, fittingly ironic, end."

With the embittered soldier finally dragged on board the helicopter, the citizens who had attended the ceremony began to depart. Only Miles, The Professor and Jack remained, their heads tilting up in unison to watch the chopper carry the prisoner away.

As luck would have it, their mutual gaze would be diverted by an unusual, almost crystalline cascade of colour spreading across the sky!

EPILOGUE

THE THREE SEASHELLS

At last, Miles was not the only one to observe what he had once believed to be a simple stream of light, which occasionally cascaded or shimmered across the sky. The thought that his once-assumed-hallucinations-now-apparent-reality were finally witnessed and realized by others, might normally have brought a smile to his face, to be followed by a sigh of relief. But instead, his facial features exhibited a mix of terror and horror. The beautiful blue sky was now partially obscured in an almost-crystalline vapour.

All three men stared at the altered sky; neither of them uttering a sound, let alone a word; and they were likely not alone. Professor Archaios, the more scientifically educated of the three, could offer no logical explanation for the phenomenon. Could the Quantubus Effect or the Cascading Convergence Phenomenon have triggered something? Could some unidentified scientists at Quantus have caused some kind of unforeseen global event in their efforts to determine how Miles had arrived in this dimension? Could Centrus have initiated a side effect, during their investigations of the same transference? Was there an undetected instability resulting in the presence of both Miles and Jack in this reality? Was this new occurrence a hint of what led to Jack's initial dimensional jump?

Whatever the cause, it was clear to them all, that there was something new for them to investigate; and it was something that they would inevitably have to deal with. This new cloud-like cover was blocking a good portion of the light and heat from the Sun, and it seemed to spread beyond the horizon, in all directions. It appeared to, quite possibly, have enveloped the world!

Just when Miles thought that his life couldn't get any more interesting, he was quickly shown the error in his beliefs.

And what of the rest of the population, did they now see it too; the ever-present change in the sky above and its potential impact on the Earth below? Were they as awash in the sea of light-grey crystalline obscurity, or were these lone men but three seashells isolated upon a shore all of their own?

Ironically enough, time would most certainly tell...

Printed in the United States
By Bookmasters